wN

SCORPION SHOWDOWN

TOM WEST

WHEELER
CHIVERS

13

This Large Print edition is published by Wheeler Publishing, Waterville, Maine, USA and by BBC Audiobooks Ltd, Bath, England.
Wheeler Publishing is an imprint of Thomson Gale, a part of The Thomson Corporation.
Wheeler is a trademark and used herein under license.

The text of this Large Print edition is unabridged.
Other aspects of the book may vary from the original edition.
Set in 16 pt. Plantin.

LIBRARY OF CONGRESS CATALOGING-IN-PUBLICATION DATA

West, Tom, 1895–
  Scorpion showdown / by Tom West.
    p. cm. — (Wheeler Publishing large print western)
  ISBN-13: 978-1-59722-579-3 (softcover : alk. paper)
  ISBN-10: 1-59722-579-7 (softcover : alk. paper)
  1. Large type books. I. Title.
PS3545.E8336S36 2007
813'.54—dc22   2007016627

BRITISH LIBRARY CATALOGUING-IN-PUBLICATION DATA AVAILABLE

Published in 2007 in the U.S. by arrangement with
Golden West Literary Agency.
Published in 2007 in the U.K. by arrangement with
Golden West Literary Agency.

U.K. Hardcover: 978 1 405 64214 9 (Chivers Large Print)
U.K. Softcover: 978 1 405 64215 6 (Camden Large Print)

Printed in the United States of America on permanent paper
10 9 8 7 6 5 4 3 2 1

SCORPION SHOWDOWN

I

Sam Moreland rode into trouble as blindly as a steer steps into quicksand. One minute his pony was drifting through the quiet night along the wagon road that snaked into Cottonwood; the next, hidden guns were spilling flame and thunder, vague forms were erupting from a rock-and-adobe structure, and all hell seemed to have broken loose.

Before the bewildered Moreland could grasp what was afoot he found himself in the vortex of a crazed melee. A rider charged out of the night, fighting to hold three wild-eyed, plunging saddle horses. Dimly, in the orange-stabbed gloom, the slack-jawed Moreland glimpsed scurrying men, .45's bucking in their fists, hauling into the empty saddles and hurricaning down the street.

In quick reaction, Moreland hurtled after them — it appeared good sense to get out of there fast. Bent low over his pony's withers, he frantically roweled the buckskin, racing in the wake of the fleeing riders. Pursuing lead whipped around him. Slugs droned and ricocheted like angry hornets. He felt a break in the rhythm of the buckskin's wild gallop. A tremor shook its barrel. It stumbled, crashed down.

Moreland found himself flying through the air. Head foremost, he hit the road, and the sun-baked ground slammed into his head like a sledgehammer. He rolled over once, carried by the impetus of his fall, then lay limp as a rag doll, blood oozing from a gash beneath his mat of hair, draining down and staining the dust. Spilled from his pockets when he dove, gold eagles were scattered all around him, gleaming dull yellow in the starlight.

When he drifted back to reality, Moreland found himself lying on a lumpy mattress, spread over a low bench. On the further side of a row of bars he focused a stable lamp, turned low, hanging from a peg on a rough adobe wall. His head felt as though it had been split with an ax and when he moved the agonizing protest of damaged neck muscles brought a protesting groan from his throat.

Sprawled on his back, he tried to force his numbed brain to function. Gradually recollection flowed back — the sudden outbreak of gunfire, the melee, his flight, the buckskin's collapse. Likely busted his conk on a rock when he was thrown, he reflected, and cautiously fingered through his hair. He flinched when he touched lacerated flesh and his fingers came away damp and sticky.

Seemed he must have butted into some kind of fracas, he cogitated; lead was flying aplenty. But where in thunder had he landed? This joint had all the earmarks of a jail.

Moreland was lengthy, loose-jointed, with the flat-planed features of the plainsman. His mop of hair was rusty red, and his eyes, a washed-out blue, held humorous lights, off-setting the belligerent set of his jaw. His garb stamped him a saddlebum — hickory shirt too thin to stand another washing, patched pants dirt-slick with usage, cracked high boots ready to fall apart.

Teeth gritted against the protest of his damaged head, he levered to a sitting position. When waves of pain subsided, he gazed curiously around the interior of an adobe. There was no doubt of his location now; the sour stench that permeated every jail was heavy on the stale air.

He saw that four cells had been built into the adobe, two on either side, a passageway running between. The far end of the passageway was blocked by a stout plank door, braced with iron straps. He was in a cooler for sure, he considered dolefully, but how in creation had he got there?

Then he became aware that the adjoining cell had an inmate, a burly slouch of a man with broad, amiable features, in puncher rig. A mass of braised flesh buried the big man's right eye and dry blood crusted a corner of his mouth. Hunkered against the bars, he was regarding his fellow prisoner with whimsical amusement.

"This the cooler?" croaked Moreland.

"It sure ain't the Ritz, pard, but then they don't nick a gent for room and board in this joint."

"How in hell did I land here?"

"They drug you in, an hour or so back."

"For what?"

The big puncher chuckled. "Wal, there was some talk of a bank heist. Seeing you're tied up with the Garrote Gang you should know."

"You loco?" snapped Moreland. "I was riding into town, peaceful as a pup on a warm brick, when lead starts splashing. A slug downs my bronc. The fall puts out my light. I wake up in this stinking joint."

"It's a good story, pard" — the other

prisoner's voice held good-natured amusement — "but you'll never made it stick. Guess you jest played out of luck. Me, I'll collect seven days for drunk and disorderly. You'll draw life, maybe the rope. Ain't a judge in the state of Texas who wouldn't throw the book at a member of the Garrote Gang."

"Quit hurrahin' me!" threw back Moreland irritably.

"When you quit spreading the bull," retorted the other. "Didn't your bunch hit the National Bank and warn't you knocked out of the saddle making a getaway?"

Light began to dawn in Moreland's mind. He'd ridden plumb into a bank heist — the Garrote Gang always hit nights. In the darkness, enraged citizens had tagged him as one of the gang. And he'd thought Lady Luck was finally on his side after that big poker game in San Antone. He'd peddled his watch for five dollars and sat in. When the game wound up at sunrise, his pockets were stuffed with more gold eagles than he'd ever believed existed. Forthwith, he'd cut across country, heading for Cottonwood, the nearest settlement, to invest in a new outfit. And he'd ridden into — this!

II

Beyond the iron-braced door, another two-man conference was taking place in the sheriff's office. Slacked at a cigarette-scarred desk, Sheriff Mark Richter resembled nothing so much as a graying bald eagle: hairless skull, long nose, and scrawny neck. Faded eyes, sunk deep below bony ridges, were bright now with satisfaction.

Nearby, spread over a straightback chair, Deputy Tod Carson, a quirley slack between thick lips, bovine features blank, absorbed the sheriff's talk. Carson, a heavy-set workhorse, with small bloodshot eyes and lumpy cheekbones, went more to brawn than brain. His chief functions were handling drunks and serving as listening post while the garrulous old sheriff resurrected past memories.

"Reckon this is a big break for me," ruminated Richter, puffing a blackened corncob pipe. "It'll sure squash talk that Mark Richter's slowing down. The Garrote Gang buffaloed every sheriff in the state but me."

The damned old wart hog was just plumb lucky, thought Carson morosely. If the banker's wife hadn't been out sitting with a sick sister and headed back home near midnight, Richter would never have known that the gang was in town. The woman had found her husband missing and hightailed for help. Aloud, he inquired stolidly, "What's so special about this Garrote Gang?"

"You learn to read and keep up with things and you'd be a heap more useful around here," returned the sheriff irately. "The Garrote Gang's the worst pack of wolves ever to plague Texas." The old lawman settled himself more comfortably in his chair. "Story is that there's four of the lobos, though it's now plain there's five. They been rampagin' through the state, heisting banks and creating hell, and they sure got a method all their own. A string of garrotings, a string of heists, and yet not one decorates a dodger."

"How come?" interjected Carson, striving to register intelligent interest.

"They never leave a witness alive. Their M.O., as the Pinkerton boys name it, is simple. They case a town, locate the bank manager's home, slide in and grab the poor bustard after nightfall, like they did George Meredith. Then they hustle the hairpin down to his bank, make him open up, clean out the vault, strangle the hombre with a leather whang — that's garroting — and hightail. It's one hell of a way to die. I

13

gamble jest thought of that bunch gives bankers nightmares."

"Guess Meredith won't get no more nightmares," said Carson absently, wondering how soon he could duck out and down a quick one at the Alamo.

"Wal, the sidewinders never got away with it in Cottonwood," continued Richter complacently, knocking the dottle out of his pipe.

"The bank's busted wide open. Ain't that getting away with it?"

"You forgot the prisoner? The colt's young; he'll break easy. When he spills his guts we got the gang and the loot, maybe."

"Sure have!" agreed the deputy and stirred restlessly. "Mind if I duck out, Sheriff? Got a little business down the street."

"Lapping up rotgut!" snapped Richter. "Nope, you go haul out that rattlesnake we jugged. The hombre should be in a fit state to talk by now."

The hinges of the heavy door to the lockup grated and the heads of both prisoners swiveled. The beefy deputy entered and clumped to the gate of Moreland's cell. Selecting a key from a metal hoop, he inserted it in the lock and threw the gate open.

"Rattle your hocks!" he grunted, plainly

in no good humor.

Moreland rose from the bench and stepped toward the open gate. His surroundings spun in a giddy whirl. Tottering like a drunk, he clutched at the lawman to maintain balance. The deputy's bunched fist swung, took the reeling prisoner beside the jaw. Moreland went down like a pole-axed steer and lay limp on his back, eyes closed, blood draining from the reopened scalp wound, splotching the tangle of his rusty hair.

"You belong in a slaughter house, Carson," commented his fellow prisoner, peering between the bars of his cell. He spat with disgust.

"Button up, or I'll work you over," growled the deputy. "The bustard offered resistance, didn't he?" He nudged the inert form with a boot toe, reached down, hooked blunt fingers beneath the unconscious man's knotted bandana and casually dragged him down the passageway, by the neck.

The sheriff ripped out a disgusted oath when his deputy entered the office through the rear door, unconcernedly hauling the limp form. "You dogblasted jackass," snapped Richter, "the hairpin's no use to us dead."

"He ain't dead," rumbled Carson. He

loosed his hold and the body thudded to the floor. "I clobbered him — self-defense."

"Clobbered him! You likely killed him," barked the sheriff, his tone brittle with anger. He jerked up from the chair, stepped quickly across the floor, dropped down on one knee and fingered the prisoner's pulse.

"Take him back," he directed, straightening, "and cut out the rough stuff. He check out you turn in your badge." His voice shrilled with anger. "I'm good and sick of you beating up prisoners."

Muttering protest, the burly deputy bent, lifted his victim's slack form, slung it across a shoulder as if it were a sack of oats and stalked out of the office.

When Moreland again became conscious of his surroundings the jail was darkened. Brain still fuzzy, he lay eyeing a small window cut high in the adobe wall, framing twinkling stars.

Remembrance of the deputy's brutality flowed into his mind and he tautened with anger. There was no doubt about it now, he reflected somberly; the law had him pegged as a member of the Garrote Gang and there was just no way he could prove his innocence. Who'd vouch for a wandering cowhand? And who'd give a damn if he

16

swung? He wasn't even in shape to make a break. If the joint was wide open he likely wouldn't have strength enough to stagger outside. Finally, he drifted off into uneasy sleep.

The rattle of a key awoke him. He sat up on the bench, blinking. A shaft of light from the rising sun speared through the small window and lanced through the obscurity of the jail. Beyond the bars of his cell he glimpsed a bald-headed aging man, a sheriff star pinned to his loose-hanging vest, who stood watching him cold-eyed. The big deputy was swinging the gate open. In the adjoining cell, the drunk-and-disorderly was still snoring.

"Jingle your spurs!" grunted the deputy.

Moreland lifted his legs off the bench and came cautiously to his feet. To his relief, the vertigo had left him, but the gash on his head burned like slow fire and his jaw felt as though it were unhinged.

He moved to the gate, stepped outside. Before he realized the deputy's intent, Carson grabbed both arms from behind and thrust them forward. Adroitly, the sheriff whipped out a pair of handcuffs and snapped them on his wrists. The deputy's big paw dropped on a shoulder and shoved him down the passageway.

Beyond the heavy door, the prisoner found himself in what was plainly the law office. Wanted notices decorated one wall, ticketed gunbelts hung from pegs, and an ancient rolltop desk stood below a window. Several straightback chairs were scattered around.

The deputy steered him to the center of the office and left him standing, while the bald-headed sheriff dropped down on a chair at the desk. Plainly bored, the beefy Carson closed the rear door and propped himself against it.

"Wal," rasped Richter, "you ready to talk?"

"About what?"

"Maybe I should slap some sense into the jasper," growled Carson.

"Button up!" retorted the sheriff, with scant patience.

Addressing the prisoner again, he advised curtly, "Quit running a blazer, mister. We got you cold. Give us the lowdown on your pards and you'll save your neck. Act stubborn and you'll swing, just as sure as God made little apples."

"You tangled your spurs," protested the prisoner. "I was riding into town when I bull into this fracas. I'm high-tailing when

18

my buckskin drops. Next I wake up in the cooler."

"So that's your story!" Richter eyed him, frowning. "Wal, I'll prove you a liar, right now." He slid open a drawer of his desk, lifted out a cardboard box, tilted it. A cascade of gold and silver coins jingled musically onto the desktop. "Six hundred and twenty dollars in gold, forty-seven in silver," he announced; "coin you grabbed in the bank. Your pards got away with a heap more."

"I won that dinero in a poker game."

"You win this in a poker game, too?" Richter held up a buckskin whang, rolled up and knotted. He untied it, dangled it distastefully, as though it were a dead snake.

"Nope!" The prisoner's features creased into a drawn smile. "I pack them whangs to fix breakages; my rig's falling apart. There's more in my saddlebags."

"You wouldn't have used one to garrote George Meredith down at the bank last night?"

"Quit funnin'!"

"Folks around Cottonwood don't figure it funny," bit back the sheriff. He carefully stowed the thong in a desk drawer, then sat eyeing the prisoner. "Gold spilling out of your pockets, yet you claim you lace your

19

rig together with leather whangs. Does that make good sense?"

"I only raked in the dinero two nights back."

"Let's quit sidestepping!" Richter's tone softened to quiet persuasion. "You ride with the Garrote Gang, you help heist the bank, you garrote the banker. You know it, we know it. Act sensible, turn state's evidence, spill your guts, and maybe, jest maybe, I can ease you out of this tight." His voice hardened. "Act ornery, you swing."

"Mister," returned the prisoner wearily, "every word I've spoken is gospel truth. You're barking up the wrong tree."

The sheriff shrugged. "Chew it over," he suggested, rising. "You got nothing to gain by acting dumb except a rope." He turned to the burly deputy. "Lock him up! I'm dropping down the street for a bite of breakfast." His tone brittled. "You muss up the hairpin and I'll lift your badge."

Cold apprehension and a feeling of utter hopelessness gripped the prisoner as the angular sheriff stalked to the doorway and the burly deputy stood eyeing him, pleased anticipation in his surly eyes. Moreland had already had a taste of the methods the big buffalo employed and he didn't savor being left to his mercy. Handcuffed, he had little chance to protect himself.

When the door slammed behind the sheriff, Carson moved toward him, hamlike fists slowly bunching. "Now we're through playing games," he growled. "You gonna talk, or do I beat that confession out of you?"

"I got nothing to confess."

"Maybe I can change your ideas," and the deputy grinned.

With growing desperation, the prisoner watched his captor's slow approach. When he came within arm's length, the big deputy swung suddenly at the damaged jaw. Moreland ducked, dodged and swung up his right leg. His sharp-toed riding boot took the beefy lawman in the groin. With an agonized grunt, Carson jackknifed. Taut-featured, Moreland interlocked the fingers of both hands. The steel cuffs rattled as he jumped forward, chopping down on the back of the deputy's bull neck. Carson crumpled like a punctured waterbag, dropped and lay feebly squirming.

Moreland stared at the burly form writhing at his feet. He should boot the daylights out of the hombre, he told himself, but somehow he couldn't use his boots on a helpless man. He backed away, stood debating his next move, impaled on the horns of a dilemma. If he ran, the manacles would be a sure giveaway. He'd be grabbed before he'd moved a dozen paces down the street. If he stuck around until the deputy picked himself off the floor, the burly lawman would likely beat him to a mash.

Carson banished the problem by slowly levering to his feet. Small eyes venomous, he reached for a chair. Gripping the back with both hands, he raised the chair shoulder-high in front of him. Behind this shield, he began stealthily shuffling toward the prisoner. Then, beyond the range of Moreland's boots, he smashed the chair down, aiming at the other's head. The prisoner crouched, raised his arms to ward off the blow. The whirling chair crashed down upon his left arm and shoulder — splintered from the impact. Left side numbed by the force of the blow, Moreland staggered, sank down upon his knees. Then the enraged deputy was at him, cursing, stamping, kicking at his face and head. Moreland rolled, shackled wrists covering his face. Mouthing incoherent curses, his assailant followed, booting viciously. With a thump, Moreland's twisting form came up against a side wall. This was the end, he thought hopelessly. This crazed lawman would stomp him to death.

III

A scream lanced into the prisoner's ears and the slogging impact of the boots suddenly ceased. Through a scarlet haze he focused a girl standing on the threshold of the street door, staring at his bloodied features with wide-eyed horror. She wore the apron and white cap of a waitress and held a metal tray covered with a white napkin. Her hair, raven-black, was brushed smooth and gathered in a bun at the back of her neck. She was trim-figured, with faint freckles and a pert nose above warm, full lips. There was a freshness, a wholesomeness about her that was like a sweet cooling breeze sweeping into the stale, fetid atmosphere of the dingy law shack.

Then he saw the horror in her gray eyes spark into fiery indignation. "You filthy, cowardly bully!" she exploded, glaring at the big deputy. With a curse, he swung toward her.

Without hesitation, she flung the tray and its contents full into his scowling features. Hot coffee running off his face and dripping from his shirt, he backed away, while tin mugs and dishes clattered to the floor and a mishmash of gruel decorated his front. She scooped up the white cloth and dropped on her knees beside the prisoner, dabbing at the blood draining from his hair.

A shadow darkened the doorway. The sheriff strode in. He checked abruptly, frosty gaze flicking from the deputy's sulky face to the mess on the floor and the girl kneeling beside Moreland's lumped form.

"Tod," he finally inquired, "how come you didn't obey orders?"

The deputy stood scowling, saying nothing.

The sheriff's tone brittled. "Drop your badge on the desk, get out — and stay out!"

"And keep out of Hogan's Diner," put in the girl tartly, and came to her feet. "I'm going to find Doc Harvey. This boy is badly injured."

"He's a killer!"

"Is that any reason to torture him?" she flashed, and tip-tapped from the office.

During the weeks that followed, life bore the aspects of a never-ending nightmare to Sam Moreland. True, there was an end to the manhandling, but, pacing a dirt-floored cell, facing charges of armed robbery and • murder, he found it hard to believe that this was reality. Some day, it seemed, he must recover, find that his brain had been deranged by a touch of the sun and the whole thing a ghastly fantasy. He never saw the pert waitress again, never saw anyone except an occasional drunk thrown into one of the cells, and a newly appointed deputy who brought his meals.

All doubt was dispelled, however, when the trial date arrived. Hunched on a chair in the crowded courtroom, the irons on his wrists and ankles rattling every time he restlessly changed position, he listened to the evidence and realized with growing hopelessness that his flight, the gold in his possession, and the rawhide whang combined to fashion a noose.

But the sentence was life imprisonment.

Folks agreed that he only escaped hanging because the lawmen still nursed hopes that he would crack and reveal the identity of the four members of the dread Garrote Gang who were still at large.

In due course he was delivered to the Walls, the gray-towered, grim old Huntsville Penitentiary, to join the somber community of the living dead.

Confined behind the high walls of Huntsville, sunk in a fog of apathy, the prisoner had plenty of time to think. There was only one way to prove his innocence, he pondered, and that was by securing the testimony of a member of the Garrote Gang.

The idea seemed fantastic. How could a felon, serving a life term, track down a renegade gang? Even if he were free, what possibility would there be of his succeeding where lawmen throughout the entire state had failed? The idea of clearing his name became a fixation.

Huntsville had its prison breaks, mostly futile. Now and then, however, a daring or desperate man went over the wall and vanished. If others could break out of Huntsville, so could he, decided Moreland. He'd bide his time and watch for the opportunity. Something told him that sooner or later it would come.

Hope reborn, he began to take an active interest in his surroundings, storing up information that might serve when his day arrived. There were plenty of "bad actors" in Huntsville, troublemakers who spent more time in solitary than out, and were close-watched by club-toting guards. On the other hand, the "trusties," well-behaved, obedient, deferential, drew the more agreeable chores and were allowed a measure of freedom behind the walls. So Moreland made "trusty" status his goal.

Weeks stretched into months, months into years, but the longed-for chance of escape never offered. Moreland still watched and waited. A model prisoner, he now had a choice billet — member of the prison fire crew. Beyond occasional drills, the fire crew had little to do except sit around the stone firehouse.

Close upon five years had dragged past when the big fire broke out. It was night when the tolling of the alarm bell awoke Moreland. When they ran the two brass hand-pumpers out into the yard the stench of burning was strong and threads of smoke issued lazily from the open windows of the square rock-and-adobe structure that housed the prison's mattress factory.

Hoses connected, the pumpers began their metallic clanking, and two streams of water poured into the building.

Quickly, it became apparent that the conflagration was beyond control. Likely it had been smoldering for hours, reflected Moreland, one of a sweating crew working a pump. There were scores of finished mattresses in that building and tons of inflammable material.

Dense smoke shrouded the prison yard now and flames began licking above the roof of the building. A frenzied clamor cascaded from the cell blocks — hundreds of penned convicts yelling, stamping, rasping metal waste buckets across the bars of their cells.

The prison gates swung back and helmeted volunteer firemen from town ran their big pumper into the yard.

They had scarcely gone into action when the roof of the factory collapsed with a dull roar. Swirling smoke veiled the yard; sparks showered high; blasting heat drove the choking firefighters back.

Eyes sore and reddened from the acrid smoke, gasping for breath as the fumes bit into his throat, Moreland retreated with the rest. Then, in the swirling smoke fog, he stumbled and fell over the body of a Huntsville fireman. The man lay limp, eyes closed, apparently overcome by smoke. A curved red metal helmet shaded his features and a heavy canvas jacket draped his shoulders.

Inspiration hit Moreland with the impact of a slug. This was his chance — at last! He darted a quick glance around. The yard was a smoke-shrouded pandemonium, through which men dabbed like gray ghosts. The roar of the flames mingled with the clamor from the cell blocks. One pumper, faint in the obscurity, was wetting down the walls of adjacent buildings. The others had apparently been abandoned in the rush for safety.

Dropping down again beside the sprawled form, Moreland quickly yanked off the unconscious man's helmet and stripped off his canvas coat. Pulling off his own striped jacket and pants, he began rapidly switching garb. The smoke was thicker now and the windows of the blazing mattress factory squares of somber scarlet. High above the doomed building great tongues of flame twisted and curled.

Eyes watering, throat parched, eyebrows singed, Moreland headed for the main gate at a run. It was open, an armed guard posted on either side. He loped up to the nearer guard. "I'm hightailing for a saw-bones," he croaked. "Smoke knocked three of our boys out already."

The guard nodded brusquely.

Moreland ducked through the gateway, dropping to a brisk walk, gratefully inhaling fresh air and marveling at the ease of his getaway. For years he'd dreamed of break-ing out of the Walls, but never of walking out.

Frame houses showed vague in the night, knots of townsfolk standing around them, staring in the direction of the prison. More-land turned. A black pall of smoke lay low over the penitentiary, its underside glowing sullen red from the reflection of the fire below. From a distance it seemed that the entire prison was afire. They'd never get that blaze under control until the mattress factory was gutted, reflected the fugitive. With luck, it might be hours before his absence was discovered.

Lights illuminated the front of a saloon, washing over the forms of saddle horses tied at the rail outside. Moreland fingered loose coin in a pocket of his purloined pants, and battled an impulse to step inside and swallow a drink — a drink that had been postponed for close upon five years. Through the windows he could see men playing poker and lounging at the bar. The batwings banged back and a puncher blundered out, plainly packing a full load. Evidently bound for an outhouse, he teetered around an angle of the building and began to make his uncertain way down an alley.

Moreland followed, moving quickly and quietly on the balls of his feet. He caught up with the well-liquored rider and called sharply, "Hey!" The puncher, as tall as himself, swung clumsily around. Moreland hit him hard, on the point of the jaw. With a grunt, the victim flopped backward, hit the ground and lay unmoving.

"Sorry, pard!" murmured Moreland. "I got no time to be choosy."

For a second time that night he traded garb.

Minutes later, in no haste, he sauntered

out of the alley. At its mouth he paused to make a quick survey of his surroundings, after which he drifted over to the hitchrail and loosed the reins of a lean black horse. Quietly, he led it away from the lights of the saloon. Fighting an urge to hurry, he checked the cinches and adjusted the stirrups. Then he set a foot in an unfamiliar stirrup and swung awkwardly into leather. The black, at the feel of an unfamiliar hand, essayed a few protesting crowhops. To his gratification, Moreland found that he had not forgotten how to stick to a saddle, any saddle. His mount settled down to a steady jog-trot and its rider headed out of town. Lady Luck, he reflected, was atoning for her misdeeds.

IV

The sun was high when a dust-plastered rider, forking a black, splashed across the broad, torpid Rio Grande. On the far bank dumpy adobes botched the saltbrush, huddled together like a flock of plump prairie hens.

Almost a week had elapsed since Sam Moreland walked out of the Walls and made his break for freedom, a week of hard riding and furtive dodging, skirting settlements and snatching meals at lonely ranch houses. No cow outfit ever refused to feed a man riding the grub line and few isolated settlers ever glimpsed a wanted dodger. Working steadily southwest, the fugitive headed for the border, where he would be beyond the reach of warrants and pursuing posses. Stiff and sore from the saddle, he had finally reached his goal.

Seen from across the river, with strings of scarlet chilies dangling from outjutting *vigas,* the adobes of San Dorcas, bedded in gray saltbrush, had a certain rustic beauty. At close quarters, however, the illusion was dispelled.

Threading between mud huts, Moreland emerged upon a rude plaza. He checked his mount to gaze around, squinting against sunglare. There was nothing pleasant about San Dorcas, he decided, except that it offered a refuge beyond the reach of United States law. Lean hogs and mongrel curs rooted in piled offal, naked brown buttons tumbled in the dust, stringy hens peeked around the adobes, and faded women in loose *camisas* and short red skirts labored around cooking fires beneath brush *ramadas.* Peons clad in dirty cotton pantaloons, their dusky features shaded by huge straw hats, loafed in spots of shade. Here and there a black buzzard preened on a *viga*. There was a putrid odor to the air, too, the odor of decay, that wrinkled the rider's nostrils.

Across the plaza, tied saddle horses switched at the swarming flies in front of a crumbling adobe, ancient whitewash flaking from its walls. Moreland raised his reins and drifted toward it. Closer, he read the inscription on a paint-peeling sign, LA CASA BLANCA — the white house. Wrapping the buckskin's reins around a rude hitchrail, he entered the cantina.

He paused inside the doorway, momentarily blinded by the abrupt transition from blazing sunlight outside to the subdued light that filtered through small square windows. When his vision cleared he glanced around the low-ceilinged room. A plank bar spanned the rear, at which a knot of vaqueros, squat, dark-featured men, with soiled scarlet sashes banding their waists and outsize rowels jingling from their boots, were jabbering and gesticulating. In marked contrast, a sprinkling of hard-faced Yanquis occupied small tables scattered over the dirt floor. These exchanged few words, sat listlessly nursing drinks and chewing cigarettes. Moreland's glance ran over their rugged features and trail-stained garb, noted the wariness that dwelt in their guarded eyes, the gunbelts buckled around their waists. A prime collection of lobos, he registered, every one dodging a warrant, doomed to rot in this stinking pueblo. Life was a heck more pleasant in Huntsville, if only a man wasn't walled in. No one paid him attention when he crossed the floor and bought a bottle of beer.

Bottle in hand, he looked around, then moved toward a rider drinking alone at a side table. One glance at the stranger's hard features and he knew he wouldn't be welcome company, but he needed information and the only way to gain it was to ask questions.

"Howdy!" he greeted genially, scraping up a chair on the opposite side of the table.

The other nodded noncommittally, his sharp black eyes appraising the newcomer with bleak disinterest. He was short, spare-built, hatchet features leathery. Grizzled hair curled from beneath a roll-brim sombrero and a cigarette dangled from his thin slit of a mouth. His holster was flared to facilitate a fast draw and its toe thonged down.

Gunshark, registered Moreland, as he thrust back his own Stetson and took a pull at the bottle of tepid beer.

"Kinda quiet around here," he commented, setting the bottle down and fishing out the makin's.

"Boothill's quieter." The gunman's voice was soft, almost gentle. "Where you from?"

"Huntsville."

The other's hatchet features creased into a silent laugh. "You're still carrying the brand."

"Come again?" requested Moreland, eyes puzzled.

"You got a prison crop," explained the other shortly. Then the fugitive understood and wondered how many more had noticed it. In prison they cut a man's hair scalp-short. His own had begun to sprout and now formed a stiff mat over his head, short and bristly as a scrub brush.

"So you busted out," mused the other. "Wal, what you figure on doing now, set around and rot?"

"I didn't bust out — I walked out. And I plan to join up with the Garrote Gang."

The gunman's leathery features creased into the parody of a grin. "You're four years too late, bucko. That bunch done busted up when you was in stir."

"I'll be doggoned!" muttered Moreland. It just didn't seem possible that the plan he had nursed for years — to locate the gang, deliver it into the hands of the law and clear his own name — had turned out to be an idle dream.

"You dead sure?" he demanded.

Amusement at his anxiety glimmered in the other's hard eyes. "They tangled their spurs in Myberg," he explained. "Buckskin O'Brien took a slug in the knee while they were making a getaway. The law corralled Buckskin and he spilled his guts to dodge the rope. Swore Dutch, the leader, always handled the garroting."

"The law round 'em up?"

"Nope!" Once started, words flowed easily from the gunman's thin lips, like water from an opened spigot. "Wells Fargo put up five thousand dollars for each, dead or alive, but the bunch just seemed to have shriveled up and blown away. Guess they quit, high-tailed out of Texas." His tone sharpened with envy. "The hairpins sure must have divvied up a sack of gold."

"Buckskin still around?"

"Thet yellow-belly drew five years," returned the gunman carelessly. "Guess he's due out. According to talk, the hombre was as mad as a drunk squaw over the deal he got from his pards. Claims they quit him cold when he was tagged, hell-bent to save their own skins, and he never got a dollar from the kitty. Swore when he got out he'd trail Dutch over the hearthstones of hell for a showdown."

"Mexico's a big place," put in Moreland, digesting all this.

"Mexico, hell!" spat out the gunman. "I'd stake my saddle they hit for the Roost."

"The Roost?" echoed Moreland, forehead corrugated.

"Culver County, Arizona Territory. Ain't a better spot in the States for a man on the lam. Lays west of the Chiricahuas. Country's pretty as a picture, they claim. A gent behave hisself, no questions asked."

The gunman crushed his butt, pushed back his chair. "Maybe I'll head thataway myself, some time. So long!"

Left alone, Moreland sat chewing over this unexpected setback. Four years too late, he thought cheerlessly. The Garrote Gang had scattered not a year after he had been incarcerated — and shattered his one chance of clearing himself of a murder charge, not to speak of a bank heist. Even if Buckskin O'Brien had denied knowledge of him, the lawmen would have figured the renegade was covering for a pard.

As he sat musing, faint hope was born. Three members of the gang were at large with a price on their heads. But he wouldn't recognize these Garrote Gang wolves if he met them face to face. And he couldn't duck into a sheriff's office and take a gander at the dodgers with the descriptions Buckskin'd likely given.

He straightened with quick decision. Better hit for this Roost than set around and slowly rot in a stinking pueblo. When he reached Arizona he'd keep his ears and eyes open. If Dutch and his pards were skulking around, sooner or later he'd get wind of them. It was a gamble, but what did he have to lose?

V

When Sam Moreland drfted into Mustang, seat of Culver County, Arizona Territory, he hit for the one saloon. The trail that wound up from the plains into the foothills of the Chiricahuas had been long and tiring. It was still early in the day and the Wagon Wheel was empty except for the paunchy barkeep and two whiskered ancients silently hunched over a checker board.

"Shot of bourbon!" said Moreland.

The apron slid bottle and glass across the bar and eyed his trail-stained garb. "Riding through?" he inquired.

"Figured on sticking around," confessed the Texan. "Seems a quiet spot."

"Ain't none quieter," agreed the barkeep. "The big news right now is the new waitress that come to town. A looker! I gamble business picks up in the Good Eats." Offhand, he added, "Hear the sheriff could use a deputy."

Moreland's lips twisted. "Guess I just wouldn't qualify."

"Could be Jim Robinson would figure different," came back the barkeep. "Around here we don't look to see if there's any dust on a man's backtrail. You'll find Jim across the Square."

Moreland sipped his drink, considering this unexpected opening. He swallowed the remnants of his drink, dropped a coin on the bar and jingled toward the batwings.

"You brace Jim!" the apron threw after him.

Outside, he paused beneath the wooden canopy, building a smoke. Mustang sure had turned out different from what he'd expected. The sleepy little settlement just didn't have the earmarks of an outlaw hideaway. Unlike the cowtowns to which he was accustomed, it lacked the usual Main Street; indeed, it lacked any street at all. A cluster of wooden buildings, mainly roofed with corrugated iron, were set around a stretch of bare ground, which he guessed must be the plaza, after the style of a Mexican pueblo. On the side where he stood were the business buildings, their paint flaking, awnings sagging, worn plank-walks splintering. To his right sprawled a barnlike structure labeled GENERAL STORE. Beyond it, divided by an alley, stood a barber shop, striped pole slanting from its front. Next came a butcher shop, with banging screen door.

On his other side steamy windows marked an eating house, sided by the Mustang Hotel, an elongated board-and-batten building. The row ended with a vacant store, its front rough-boarded up.

Northward of the square was lumped the gray bulk of a livery barn, and to the south reared the only imposing building in town, the Culver County Courthouse, a two-storied, narrow-windowed plank and adobe structure.

All were overshadowed and dwarfed by the vista to the east. Here the Chiricahuas blocked out the horizon, a stupendous backdrop carved by a million years of volcanic activity. By bench and cliff and spur, the erosion-chiseled mass rose higher and yet higher, culminating in lofty peaks whose naked summits, wreathed with fleecy garlands of cloud, thrust high into the blue.

But Moreland's interest was not in scenery, but in a peeled log cabin, standing alone, across the square. Squinting, he read the sign over its door: SHERIFF'S OFFICE. Plunked solid and unmoving on a chair tilted against its front was the chunky form of a man. Sunlight glinted upon a metal badge affixed to his dark shirt.

That, decided Moreland, would be the sheriff, and the sheriff needed a deputy — no questions asked. His dinero was running short and it was plain he'd have to rustle up some kind of job. His lips curved with inward amusement at thought of rodding the law; yet what better way to locate the fugitive members of the Garrote Gang? he reasoned. Behind a law badge he could poke around at will. But still he hesitated. It was hard to forget that he was on the lam, and the instinctive fear of the hunted held him back.

He crushed the cigarette beneath a heel, loosed the reins of his tied pony, mounted and jogged across the square.

As he approached the law shack, his qualms strengthened. This lawman looked tough, tough right through. His close-cut hair was thinning and a sun-faded moustache drooped over lips, clamped on the stem of a pipe, that came together as tight

41

as the jaws of a bear trap. His head came up as Moreland drew close and the Texan looked into stony gray eyes, deep-sunk in craggy features, that held the guarded alertness found in hunters as well as the hunted. Somehow, Moreland was reminded of an old lobo who had reached the age when peace and quiet were preferable to action, but whose capacity to claw was by no means diminished.

He stepped out of leather, eyeing the blocky form warily. "Barkeep claims you need a deputy," he ventured.

The sheriff sat motionless, puffing his pipe, eyes, blunt as bullets, probing his visitor.

"Where you from?" he inquired at length.

"Texas."

"What was the charge?" He raised a hand as protest leaped to the rider's lips. "Quit fretting! I never was interested in the amount of dust on a man's backtrail, but" — a note of bleakness crept into his tone — "it sure better be clean just as long as he's around here. The job pays seventy-five dollars a month."

"Suits me," said Moreland.

"Stable that cayuse in the barn out back," Robinson told him, coming to his feet. "I'll dig out a badge. We'll tend to the swearing

42

in later."

It was as easy as that! Within an hour of riding into Mustang, Moreland — to his amazement — found himself packing a deputy sheriff badge.

In high good humor he booked a room in the board-and-batten hotel. He'd sure drawn aces, he reflected. Fellow never knew which way a frog would jump.

He moved in front of a mirror, with faded gilt frame, hung over the washstand in the boxy hotel room, eyeing the metal star pinned to his shirt. Now he could circulate around and dig into the records of the assortment of wanted men who had taken refuge in Culver County. If his luck continued to hold, he stood a gambling chance of clearing his name and maybe latching onto one or two of the five thousand dollar bounties put up by Wells Fargo for arrest and conviction of members of the elusive Garrote Gang.

As the thrill began to wear off an emptiness beneath his belt reminded him that he hadn't eaten since sunup. He gave the badge a swipe with his sleeve to improve its luster, grabbed his hat and headed for the street.

It was midafternoon when he brushed aside the grimy fly curtain draping the doorway of Ed Sayers' Good Eats. The place was empty. Slapping his hat on a peg, he slid onto one of the round stools set along the counter.

A trim, raven-haired girl stepped out from behind a partition in the rear. Moreland eyed her with approval, then suddenly had a feeling that he'd met this girl some place before. Brow creased, his glance ran over her fresh features — pert nose, faint powdering of freckles, warm red lips — striving to place her. Her gray eyes met his, dropped to the badge on his shirt.

"Well," she said caustically, "this must be the age of miracles. Weren't you sentenced to life imprisonment at Cottonwood, back in Texas?"

Then he remembered — the big deputy booting hell out of him in the Cottonwood sheriff's office, a girl's scream, the waitress standing by the doorway, the soft sympathy in her big gray eyes as she dabbed at his bloody face.

"So you're the gal!" he exclaimed and grinned. "That was me, ma'am, and I never did get a chance to thank you, but I'm sure doing it now. Reckon you saved my life."

"I doubt if it was worth saving," she returned with cool indifference. "They should have hanged you. Well, I suppose you broke jail." She lifted her shoulders. "Most every good-for-nothing finds his way to this renegade roost sooner or later."

"Listen!" he begged. "I was innocent. I was just —"

"That's what they all say," she threw back resignedly. "Save your breath — just give me your order."

Later she banged down a plate on which reposed a sizzling steak, fried potatoes and onions, then served his coffee and stalked away.

Left alone, Moreland went to work on the steak, but somehow he seemed to have lost his appetite. He couldn't keep his mind off the waitress and the disgust in her gray eyes.

Finally, he pushed his empty plate aside, lit a cigarette and sat staring glumly out at the sun-swept plaza. His indifference vanished as a girl sauntered past, carrying several books in the crook of an arm. A slim girl, moving with a willowy grace that not even the somber dark dress she wore, its flowing skirt brushing the tops of button shoes, the bodice buttoned high in the neck, could conceal. Her features were pale, finely textured, a perfect oval, and her straight nose had an imperious lift. This, with the firmness of her lips, gave her an expression of regal disdain. Sam Moreland thought she was just about the most attractive girl he had ever seen.

He was so entranced, following her progress, that he was unaware that the waitress had emerged from behind the partition again.

"Your eyeballs are bulging," she remarked, her tone edged.

Moreland released a deep breath and turned. "That gal is sure a sight for sore eyes."

"And knows it!" she retorted. "The belle of Mustang!"

"Who in creation is she?"

"Phyllis Robinson, the sheriff's daughter, our dedicated schoolma'am," she told him curtly. "Otherwise, the Empress."

"Don't seem to be a friend of yourn."

The waitress snorted. "To that stuck-up vamp, I'm dirt. All she's interested in is collecting scalps. She'll get yours!"

"You wouldn't be a mite jealous?"

She tossed her head and stepped back into the kitchen, out of sight.

VI

Sheriff Robinson and his new deputy slacked in chairs tilted against the front of the law shack, killing time — their usual occupation.

It seemed to suit the sheriff, reflected Moreland, but although he hadn't worn the star for a week yet, he was conscious of a growing restlessness. Adding another butt to the litter around his chair, he yawned, a protracted yawn, indicating utter boredom, and the old straightback chair creaked as he restlessly changed position.

Robinson puffed his blackened briar, as unmoving as a cigar store Indian. Moreland fished out the makin's and began wearily to fashion another smoke. Before them, across the square, Mustang lay outspread, a picture of sluggish serenity bathed in warming sunlight — just as it was yesterday, would be tomorrow, and likely every day till Eternity, considered the deputy, with gloomy disgust. "Doggone it," he complained, "don't anything ever happen around here?"

"That should be no cause for complaint, Sam." Robinson's deep, controlled voice held mild rebuke. "The way I see it, a sheriff is elected to keep the peace. This is likely the most peaceful county in Arizona Territory, which is how folks crave it to be, else why would they reelect me as regular as the sun rises? Over in Lennox County, old Sheriff Lanker got a dozen deputies scattered around, while I got one. Lanker averages a shoot-out a week; we ain't had a killing in a coon's age. Show me another town in these United States where they got no use for a jail."

For once the sheriff was in a talkative mood, thought Moreland. Aloud, he agreed grudgingly. "Guess you got 'em broke to harness."

"The Good Book says, 'Forgive and ye shall be forgiven,' " continued Robinson, his voice deepening with conviction. "When a man enters Culver County his iniquities are forgiven. He'll get what's coming when he steps through the Golden Gates and St. Peter tallies his misdeeds in the Big Book. As for me, his record is no concern of mine. Like I heard a preacher say, 'The past is dead, forget it.' " He knocked the dottle out of his pipe. "What in thunder you kicking about? You crave trouble?"

"I guess not," returned the Texan, "but I'm cultivating seat sores. They itch!"

"You prefer saddle sores, with a posse eating your dust?" A caustic note had crept into the sheriff's voice.

"Nope."

"Wal, maybe you should button your lip."

The new deputy said nothing. He was loco, he told himself, to stir Robinson up. According to stories that circulated, there was dynamite beneath that stolid exterior.

Musing, the deputy decided that he just didn't savvy Robinson. It was sure a tribute to the old buffalo, he reflected, that the county should be literally without crime, despite the fact that there were more renegades on the loose than in all the rest of the Territory combined. As the gunshark had claimed in San Dorcas, it was a wanted man's paradise.

One slack evening in the Wagon Wheel, Baldy, the fleshy barkeep, had explained how Sheriff Robinson, with the hearty cooperation of all concerned, handled law enforcement officers and bounty hunters. The sheriff received them all with impassive courtesy. He carefully scrutinized any wanted dodger the visitor might produce, declared gravely that the hombre described thereon was a complete stranger and invited the lawman to poke around for himself. Word went swiftly to the wanted man. An army could have hidden in the spiderweb of ravines and coulees that lay around Mustang, and the quarry would duck out of sight. Usually, the hunter looked around for two or three days, then pulled out with tight-lipped frustration.

Bounty hunters received somewhat different treatment, explained Baldy, as befitted measly coyotes hunting men down for blood money. In a dozen different ways they would be reminded that they were in hostile territory. Their ponies would mysteriously slip macarties and wander away; salt would find its way into the sugar shaker in the Good Eats; the price of a shot of bourbon would jump up to a dollar; burrs would find their way beneath saddles and drive the bounty hunter's bronc into spasms of frenzied bucking. If all this failed, a rattlesnake might be found coiled on his bed at the hotel. Most got the message and quickly beat it.

It was a crazy situation, considered Moreland, but then Culver was a crazy county — and likely the most law-abiding in the West. If and when he located members of the Garrote Gang he'd have to watch his step, or he'd likely get the treatment, too.

In the meantime, it seemed he was destined to set, and set, and set.

It was around noon when the stranger rode in, grimed with trail dust and forking a grulla. From habit, both lawmen weighed him as his mount jogged across the square, its hooves stirring small swirls of slow-settling dust. And Moreland guessed that a slew of sharp eyes followed his progress, too, for no stranger entered Mustang unmarked, and plenty of feet would be itchy until his identity was established.

He was wire-thin, with a long stubbled jaw, black hair curling in a ragged fringe beneath his battered sombrero. He wore black corduroys, plaid shirt and a sleeveless vest. A faded red bandana hung loose around his throat and he rode straight in the saddle, like a cavalryman.

Steering the grulla to the water trough outside the saloon, he allowed it a short drink, then tied to the rail. Stiff from the saddle, he moved slowly toward the batwings, pushed through and disappeared inside the saloon.

Moreland noted that he walked with a marked limp and that his holster was worn on the left side — and tied down.

"A gunny," commented the deputy, "and I gamble he served a hitch with Uncle Sam's Cavalry."

The sheriff nodded, saying nothing.

"Invalided out, maybe," added Moreland, remembering the limp.

Robinson raised his blocky shoulders with an unconcerned shrug. "Maybe! More likely on the dodge. I'll brace the hombre — later." With that, he tapped his pipe against a chair leg and came to his feet. "Guess I'll ramble down to the house. Door latch sticks, promised the gal I'd fix it." More-land watched his stocky form plug around the angle of the law shack; then he returned to watching the saloon, with little interest. He saw the newcomer limp out, step into leather again and angle off toward the livery. A short time later he emerged, saddlebags slung across a shoulder, and headed for the hotel.

He was sure no saddlebum, decided the deputy, or he would have stretched out on the straw pile in the livery for the night. Then Moreland dozed off to sleep.

He awoke with a start, jerked out a fat silver watch and consulted it. School was due to be let out.

Rising hastily, he hit across the hoof-packed square, ducked through an alley and came out on a brushy flat. Following a winding trail through the brush, he passed shacks and corrugated-roofed cabins. Beyond them sat a little square schoolhouse, surmounted by a bell tower and painted a sun-faded red. At the gate of the school yard, he hunkered, made a smoke and set himself to wait.

The door of the schoolhouse burst open and a dozen or so youngsters erupted. Moreland straightened and smiled as they tornadoed past him. Phyllis Robinson followed. She paused to lock the door, then composedly descended the wooden steps.

The new deputy couldn't deny that he'd fallen for her, hook, line and sinker. But the fascinating Miss Robinson was a tantalizing young woman who was adept at keeping her admirers dangling. From the first she had impressed upon the admiring Moreland that she had no matrimonial intentions, that she felt it was her duty to keep house for her father, a widower.

"Howdy, Phyllis!" he hailed, advancing across the yard. "Another day, another dollar!"

"Hello, Sam!" she returned, flashing a mechanical smile.

"There's a stranger in town," he volunteered, dropping in beside her.

"Indeed!"

"And your paw's fixing the latch."

"Fixing — what?" She eyed him sharply.

"Ain't your door latch sticking?"

"Oh — yes!"

"That's big news in Mustang," he told her wryly, but the girl seemed preoccupied. Conversation languished as they moved through the brush.

When Moreland had escorted Miss Robinson home, the thought struck him that it might be a good idea to check up on the stranger and save Jim Robinson a chore.

He hit for the hotel.

Easing back a glass-paneled door, he stepped into the lobby, which was small and square, lined by shabby leather-upholstered rockers, beside each of which stood a bright brass spittoon. In the rear was a waist-high showcase on which reposed a frayed register. A keyboard hung on the wall behind it, and — between — Mrs. Larcombe, the manageress, her ample form spilling over a sturdy wing chair. Phyllis Robinson had been heard to describe her as "a sack of suet." Bulk, however, didn't limit the buxom widow's activity. She handled the duties of scrubwoman, chambermaid and washwoman, and never missed a dance. Her eyes, two snapping black buttons, were buried deep in features as rounded and soft as a ripe melon. Although her voice held a prickly sharpness, there was never an easier touch for a deadbeat.

Moreland sauntered up to the showcase, nodded offhandedly to the manageress overflowing the chair behind it, knitting needles clicking. He swung the tattered register around and eyed the latest entry, that of *Mike Heckel, Texas.*

"This Heckel hombre, he say what brought him to Mustang?" he inquired.

"I never pry into other folks' business," retorted Mrs. Larcombe, "but I have a notion he's hunting someone."

"A lousy bounty hunter!" grunted the deputy.

"If that's the case, the boys will give him the usual treatment," said Mrs. Larcombe, with cheerful unconcern.

"Where's the jasper now?"

"In his room, sleeping, I guess. He was tuckered out."

So that was that, thought Moreland, and yawned.

With nothing to do but kill time, Moreland drifted along the plankwalk. That latch must be giving Jim Robinson trouble, he thought; he hadn't seen hide nor hair of the sheriff since noon.

At the batwings, he checked and glanced into the saloon. The drone of low-voiced talk flowed into his ears. Quiet as boothill, he registered, with lurking amusement; the stranger had the boys guessing.

By the stove, bulking in the center of the floor, the two whiskered old-timers silently pushed checkers around. A sprinkling of townsmen bellied up to the bar, among them wizened "Bigfoot" Sanders, proprietor of the livery, and Al Jarvis, the butcher, an amiable slouch of a man. By a window, Justice of the Peace Jonathan Whitestone, an accountant with an embezzlement record, alone at a table, sipped his customary two fingers of bourbon with the stiff dignity that befitted his office.

Then the deputy's glance focused on the individual responsible for this epidemic of shyness, nursing a shot of bourbon at the far end of the bar, conspicuously alone, and he knew that the stranger's eyes, restless as a lobo's, had picked him up in the backbar mirror. Heckel had hardcase stamped all over him, from his eroded features, split by a thin slit of a mouth, to the thonged-down holster. An impulse seized Moreland to brace the hombre and inquire his business in Mustang. It was a sure thing Heckel wasn't a lawman or he would have dropped into the office.

VII

All talk cut off abruptly when he pushed inside and jingled across the floor, knowing that, in the backbar mirror, the stranger followed every move. He stepped up beside the gunman and drawled, "Staying long, mister?"

"What's it to you?" The other's voice

sounded as though it had been strained through ashes.

Moreland touched the badge pinned to his shirt. "Around here we usually check up on strangers."

"I figure on punching the breeze, just as soon as I even up with a certain yellow-gutted coyote," rasped the other.

"Feud, eh?"

"Let's call it a showdown."

Tough, real tough, reflected Moreland. A calloused old lobo, likely snake-fast on the draw, itching to even up for some nagging grievance through gunsmoke. How would Sheriff Robinson have handled him? He couldn't run the jasper out of town for intentions, and likely, if he tried, the hombre would plug him before his own gun cleared the holster.

It came to him, facing his first real threat of trouble since he'd pinned on the badge, just how awkward and inexperienced he was.

"Wal, get this," he came back curtly, "we don't stand for gunplay in Culver County. You crave to bed down in boothill, just jerk that hogleg."

The stranger considered this, taking a long drink, the glass in his right hand, the left dangling over his holster. His gaze never left the rangy deputy and Moreland read caustic amusement, or maybe derision, in his dark eyes.

"Figure you could ticket me for boothill?" he inquired.

"Maybe!"

The other simply spat — and waited.

Moreland stood undecided, conscious that he had received a challenge, and that every silently-watching patron in the saloon knew it. His right fist clenched, then slackened. Odds were he couldn't slug the stranger fast enough to stop a draw. Lead would fly and, through his blundering, he would have precipitated the first shoot-out in Mustang. He could imagine Robinson's disgust. What was more, he had no right to butt in — the sheriff had said he would handle it. He might not lose his life but he surely would his badge.

A sensible man would pull out, he told himself. He'd done his job, issued a warning. So, without further word, he swung on a heel, threaded between small tables toward the batwings, feeling like a tin-canned dog and knowing that everyone present figured he'd backed away from the threat of a gun. He'd surely made an all-fired jackass of himself.

In no good humor, he trudged toward the

hotel. For weeks he'd hungered for action, he cogitated, and when the chance came he'd sidestepped it. When the story got around, he'd gamble folks would be laughing all over the county.

He banged into his room, touched a match to the wick of the oil lamp on the shabby bureau, yanked off his boots, scaled his hat into a corner and hung his gunbelt on a peg. Disgustedly, he flopped onto the bed. Some time later he blew out the lamp and drifted off to sleep. . . .

Bony fingers, digging into a shoulder, nudged him back to wakefulness. He levered to a sitting position, blinking into a stable lamp dangling from the hand of Bigfoot Sanders, the liveryman.

"Rattle your hocks!" snapped Sanders. "Someone beefed that hombre you braced back in the saloon."

"You mean — he's dead?" gulped Moreland.

"Dead as Santa Anna," grunted the liveryman, "and all spraddled out in the alley beside the general store."

A bracketed lamp, turned low, shadowed the lobby when Moreland crossed it behind Sanders. Outside, a sliver of moon laid a faint silver sheen on the sleeping settlement.

The two strode along the plankwalk,

checked at the mouth of an alley, a narrow canyon of darkness squeezed between the saloon and the general store. Here a knot of men stood silently around a limp form, stretched on its back, all but the boots in shadow.

Moreland took the stable lamp from Sanders and bent over the corpse, studying it. Heckel's mouth gaped open, and the sun-scorched features were still distorted, as though he had died in agony. The bony fingers of his right hand were latched loosely around the walnut butt of his gun, half-drawn from the holster. There seemed no sign of blood, or a bullet wound. Frowning with perplexity, the deputy bent lower, glimpsed a red weal around the dead man's throat, deep-cut, smoldering red where a choking thong had bitten in. "Hell!" he exclaimed. "The jasper was garroted."

"You don't say!" There was a note in Sanders' voice that drew Moreland's quick, frowning glance.

"Hell of a way to kill a man," he commented, and cleared his throat, irritated by its dryness.

"I'd say it was the work of a white-livered skunk," said Sanders.

Then silence draped the scene again. Moreland stood uncertainly, holding the lantern, conscious of the scrutiny of half a dozen pairs of eyes. He was the law; they were waiting for him to act. Just what in creation should he do next?

"Guess we better get the sheriff," he said awkwardly.

"He's due," a man told him. "Al Jarvis hotfooted for his place."

Fast-moving feet drummed on the plank-walk, loud in the quiet night. Sheriff Robinson's blocky form emerged into the wavering circle of light cast by the stable lamp. Big Al Jarvis, the butcher, bulked behind him.

The sheriff gave a quick glance around, nodded at Moreland, dropped on one knee beside the corpse. Moreland held the lamp close, while Robinson carefully looked the body over. He slid the .45 free of the slack fingers, pressed the release key under the gun, caught the heavy cylinder in his left hand, shook out the loads into a palm. "Five beans on the wheel," he commented. "No empties. Guess the hombre never had a chance to shoot." He dropped the shells into a pocket, replaced the cylinder, slid the key home and handed the weapon to Moreland. Then he rolled the body over, eyeing the back of the neck. Moreland saw that the red weal terminated just behind each ear.

61

"Some jasper jumped him from behind," ruminated the sheriff, "hooked a cord under his chin, maybe a rawhide thong, cut off his wind."

"A dirty killing!" grated Sanders.

"A quiet one," drawled Robinson. "A gunshot would have roused the town."

He came to his feet, stood peering around. "Any witnesses?"

"Me and Al found him," volunteered Sanders, "was heading home from the saloon. Al tripped over his boots."

"Lamp anyone around?"

"Nope!"

"Guess no one's acquainted with the jasper?"

Again there was silence. "His moniker's Heckel," put in Moreland. "Hails from Texas. I checked the hotel register."

Robinson stood eyeing the body and rasping his chin. "Someone's due to swing for this," he commented grimly, "and the skunk's in town right now."

"You said a mouthful," returned Sanders, and his glance strayed toward the deputy.

"Wal, guess I'll empty his pockets," decided the sheriff. He dropped down again and began searching the dead man. A pitiful little pile arose beside the corpse — a sagging tobacco sack, book of papers, block of stinkers, a worn wallet, jackknife, some silver coins. That was all.

Robinson slipped off the victim's red bandana and wrapped his meager possessions in it, stuffed the bundle into a pocket. Onlookers had begun to drain away.

The sheriff came to his feet. "Pack the jasper down to the barn," he told Moreland, nodding toward the body. "I'll give his room at the hotel a once-over. Meet me at the office."

He moved off briskly. Sound of his steps, hollow on the plankwalk, died with distance.

"Someone give me a hand," said Moreland.

Jarvis stepped forward, hooked beefy fingers under the armpits of the limp form. Moreland gathered up the legs. They moved slowly down the alley, heading for an old barn in the rear of the general store that did double duty as mortuary and lockup for occasional drunks.

The corpse deposited on a bench in the barn, Moreland trudged across the moonlit square, his elongated shadow reaching ahead. It was hard to realize that a man had been killed, silently, ruthlessly, while he lay sleeping, not a stone's throw distant.

He opened the office door, lit a lamp suspended from the ceiling, dropped onto a chair. There was little in the way of furnishings in the law shack, outside a plank table that served as desk and three straightback chairs. A potbellied heating stove stood near the rear wall, a few tagged handguns and rifles were heaped on a shelf, and an old oak bureau sat against a side wall, its drawers a catchall for odds and ends.

Absently, the deputy made a smoke, his thoughts still on the killing. There was a certain amount of glamour when a man went out in a blaze of gunfire, but this silent murder in the night chilled his spine. This Heckel had claimed he'd come to Mustang for a showdown. It was plain to Moreland that the man he was hunting had stalked him, quiet as a cat, when he left the saloon. He never had a show with that cord cutting into his windpipe. As Sanders had said, it was a dirty killing.

He straightened when the sheriff entered, the dead man's saddlebags dangling across one shoulder. Dropping the saddlebags on the table, Robinson pulled up a chair. First he pulled out the red bandana, bulging with the victim's personal possessions, and spilled them on the tabletop. The only one that promised to yield a clue to the killer, thought Moreland, was the wallet.

He watched closely as Robinson extracted

its contents with slow deliberation: a frayed bill of sale for the grulla, a slim wad of greenbacks, mostly twenties. Nothing more.

The sheriff knotted everything up in the bandana again, tossed it onto a shelf. Then he eased his chair around so that he faced his deputy, brought out the blackened old briar and pouch, stuffed tobacco into the bowl of the pipe, lit up. "Now," he said, deep-set eyes focusing on Moreland, "tell me what you know, all you know."

"It ain't much," confessed the deputy. "He hails from Texas. He was seeking a showdown with a certain yellow-gutted coyote, so he claimed. He was found dead in an alley, choked, throttled, strangled — you name it!"

"How come you tangled with him in the saloon?"

Moreland started. How in creation had the sheriff wised up so quickly to the saloon incident? he wondered. One of the patrons must have made it his business to give Robinson an earful. The old moseyhorn sure didn't miss much.

He shrugged. "It wasn't such-a-much. I inquired his business in town, warned him against gunplay."

"And he called your hand," put in Robinson imperturbably. "You backed away."

Moreland flushed, knowing how his actions must have looked to an onlooker.

"Wal," he admitted lamely, "the hairpin was a mite belligerent. I sidestepped gunplay, knowing how you feel about promiscuous shooting."

"He name the hombre he was hunting?"

"Nope."

Silently, the sheriff reached for the saddlebags, unstrapped one and lifted out a sheaf of wanted dodgers. Some were old and yellowed, others dated within the year. Most seemed to have been issued by Texas sheriffs. All carried rewards for the apprehension, or information as to the whereabouts, of wanted men.

Robinson spread the dodgers over the table. "Heckel was a bounty hunter, no more and no less. He rode into Mustang to collect a little blood money."

"That's not the way he laid it out," protested Moreland.

"Maybe he had a reason," threw back Robinson. "I yanked out one dodger. Take a gander at this." He brought a folded sheet from a pants pocket, opened it out, handed it to his deputy.

Moreland almost gasped when he glimpsed the reproduction of the wanted man's features on the dodger. They were his own. Numbly, he read the wording below:

$250 REWARD

will be paid for information leading to the capture of Samuel Moreland, escapee, a former member of the Garrote Gang. Age 24; height 6'11"; eyes blue; hair rusty red; weight 165.

James Murray, Warden
Huntsville Penitentiary, Texas.

"So you were tied up with the Garrote Gang!" The sheriff's tone was ominously quiet.

"Nope!" said Moreland shortly.

"You claiming the warden of Huntsville's a liar?"

"Hell, I was framed!"

Robinson laughed shortly. "I never met a jailbird who wasn't. Heckel was garroted. I say you're as guilty as hell." The sheriff's even tones held an edge now.

"I swear I never beefed the jasper," protested the deputy vehemently.

Robinson ignored him. "The way I size it up," mused the lawman, "Heckel was a bounty hunter. He read your brand in the saloon and you knew it. You skulked in the alley till he came out, jumped the jasper, garroted him and beat it to your room. According to the dodger it most likely ain't your first killing."

Moreland sat tight-lipped. For the second time, he thought bitterly, he was accused of a killing in which he had no hand. Not that he blamed the sheriff — the finger pointed straight at him. The motive was plain and he'd sure had opportunity. In the face of the wanted poster, protestations of innocence would be wasted breath. One thing only would convince Robinson — proof. That meant uncovering the real killer. The bustard was around town, and likely a member of the Garrote Gang. How in thunder could he locate the lobo?

The sheriff's voice broke into his cogitations, a trifle weary. "I'll give you a break, Sam. You better ride — and keep on riding, right out of the county."

VIII

Beat it, and there would be no doubt about his guilt, reflected Moreland. Again he would be branded a killer and, as at Cottonwood, the real murderer would escape.

"Believe me or not," he assured the sheriff earnestly, "I didn't put out Heckel's light. I wasn't even wise he packed the dodger."

Robinson said nothing, just hunched on the chair, eyeing his deputy, disbelief plain on his rugged features.

"Give me time!" begged Moreland. "I got to chew this over."

"I offer you an out," barked the sheriff, "and you got the gall to play for time. Dammit, I should slip cuffs on you right now."

"Have a heart, Jim!" begged the accused rider. "Just give me to sunup. Heck, it ain't too far off."

Robinson fingered his chin. "All right," he agreed finally, and rose. "I'll grab me a little shut-eye. If you're around when I show, the charge is murder." With that, he stumped out of the office.

Moreland sat listening to his boots crunch dust, until the sound died on the night. Left alone, he slowly made a smoke, striving to control the turmoil in his mind. Even now he found it hard to realize that he again stood in the shadow of a noose.

Branded killer again, he considered somberly, and by sufficient evidence to convince any jury in the territory. But for Robinson's forbearance he'd be under arrest right then. And with only the ghost of an out — locate the real killer. How was that possible in his three or four remaining hours of freedom?

His glance dropped to the collection of

wanted notices, strewn over the table where the sheriff had dumped them. Odds were, he mused, the killer was right there. With quickening interest, he began sifting through the dodgers, scrutinizing each long and carefully.

Dawn was close when he finally worked through the pack. Growing light, filtering through the windows, began to pale the yellow beams of the stable lamp suspended overhead.

With a tired yawn, Moreland shuffled the crackling sheets together. As the result of his labors he had set four to one side, tying them to men in town. It was logical to believe, he decided, that the killer was a townsman, someone who was sufficiently scared of the stranger to brutally terminate his life, and what greater fear could a fugitive have than that of being hauled back to the scene of his crime to swing from a rope, or face a long penitentiary term? If he had been a member of the dread Garrote Gang he had even greater cause for fear.

But time was needed to investigate these suspects and time was fast running out. Before another hour passed, the sheriff would be back — with the handcuffs.

He pushed away from the table, straightened wearily, and moved to the doorway.

Mustang still slept. Across the bare strip of the square buildings showed dim through the clinging mists of dawn. Nothing moved.

The troubled deputy's roving glance lit on the ungainly bulk of the livery barn. His attention quickened as a rider, forking a piebald pony, emerged from the gaping black square of the entrance, abruptly reined westward and angled toward the plank bridge that spanned Gold Creek, a surging stream on the far side of the settlement.

Moreland stood eyeing the horseman, dim in the vague light, until he vanished from view behind the row of wooden business structures. There seemed to be something furtive about his actions. Just who was the hairpin, wondered the deputy, and how come he was sliding out of town before anyone was likely to be stirring? Most men would have stuck around for a mug of dip and maybe some chuck before hitting the trail. He was sure no townsman: no one in Mustang forked a piebald.

With quick resolution, Moreland stepped back to the table, thrust the four wanted dodgers he had set aside into a pants pocket and headed for the livery with long, eager strides.

Loose planks rattled beneath his feet as he

stepped into the gloom of the cavernous barn. A ripe horsey stench hit his nostrils and, from the obscurity, came the rattle of a halter rope, the stamp of a restive pony.

Just inside the wide entrance, a cubbyhole, partitioned off with clapboard, served as the liveryman's sleeping and living quarters. Moreland knocked on the closed door, drew no response, turned the handle and stepped inside. Growing light, percolating through a grimy square of barn sash, revealed Ed Sanders stretched out on a truckle bed that was jammed against the rear wall. Sanders lay on his back, fully clothed except for his boots. He was apparently sound asleep, his breath whistling between loose lips.

As though triggered by the deputy's entrance, an alarm clock, set on a battered straightback chair, exploded into a tinny jangle. Moreland stood watching as the liveryman grunted sleepily, groped for the clock, cut off the alarm. Then he rolled over.

"Hey, shake a leg!" barked the deputy.

Sanders' eyes blinked open. Still drugged by sleep, he struggled to a sitting position and sat blinking at his visitor.

"Hell!" he growled. "What's itching you?"

"Who's the hombre who rode out five minutes back?"

"Why ask me?" grumbled the liveryman,

swinging his legs off the bed and reaching for his boots. "I been sleeping, and I sleep sound."

"Quit sidestepping," snapped Moreland. "He was here, I lamped the hombre."

"I jest wouldn't know." A note of sulky antagonism had crept into Sanders' tone.

"You stable a piebald last night?"

"Nope!"

"This jasper forked one."

"You can't prove nothing by me," mumbled the liveryman, and bent to lace his boots. The man was lying, covering up, thought Moreland. Why?

"Ed," he said, with slow significance. "There was a killing last night. 'Member? You covering up or jest acting ornery?"

Sanders came to his feet. Short in stature, he had to look up to meet the lanky deputy's eyes. His uneasy gaze focused on Moreland, wavered, slid away. "I don't know nothing!" he reiterated stubbornly.

"You have a hand in Heckel's killing?"

"Don't you try and pin that on me, Sam Moreland," spluttered the other. "I'm clean, and I got an alibi — Al Jarvis. There's folks who say —" He cut off at sight of the anger blazing in the deputy's eyes, hard now as bottle glass.

"That I beefed Heckel," put in Moreland.

"And you lit the fire, peddling a line of guff to the sheriff that I was faking sleep, fully dressed." By the quick uneasiness in Sanders' eyes he knew his random shot had hit the bull's-eye.

"Weren't you?" muttered the liveryman.

"You hit the hay with your duds on; does that make you a killer?"

Sanders said nothing, just stood fingering his bristly chin and shuffling his feet uneasily.

"Except," added Moreland, his tone brittle, "you had good reason to put out Heckel's light."

Ignoring the quick protest on the liveryman's lips, he yanked out the four wanted posters, selected one and read aloud, "Two hundred and fifty dollars reward. Wanted — for murder. Jonas Secker, height five foot seven, weight one forty-five. Hair gray; eyes brown; features pinched; mole below left eye. Charged with the lethal knifing of one John Hawker. Thomas Hall, Sheriff, Tucson, Arizona Territory." He thrust the yellowed dodger at the shrinking Sanders and demanded, "Wal?"

"That was six-seven years back," muttered the liveryman. "I was lickered up. The bustard grabbed for his gun."

"So you ripped him up!" mocked More-

74

land. "Now you killed again."

"You're a liar!" Sanders' voice shrilled with vehemence. "How would I know this Heckel hombre packed that dodger? I got a witness! Al Jarvis never left me all evening. Didn't we find the carcass? You brace Al — he'll back me."

"Could be you two were working in cahoots," returned Moreland softly. "Heckel packed a dodger for Jarvis, too."

"You been chewing loco weed," declared Sanders, with scowling disgust.

"That piebald still slip your memory?" threw back the deputy, reverting to his original inquiry.

"Never was no piebald in this barn," declared the liveryman, and shouldered past him to the door.

It didn't seem likely that he'd get anything more out of Ed Sanders, considered Moreland. The fact that he was a wanted man meant little; the features of likely three-quarters of Mustang's citizens decorated dodgers. But why was he covering for the rider who forked the piebald? Maybe a talk with Al Jarvis would throw some light on the problem.

It was broad daylight when Moreland stepped out of the livery. Sanders had vanished into the depths of the barn.

The deputy found Jarvis in his butcher shop, stripped down to vest and pants, busily engaged in dismembering the carcass of a steer. The butcher was a big, smooth-featured man, with an affable smile that appeared to be pasted upon his broad features. His voice was deep and melodious and he looked as inoffensive as a well-broken workhorse. But Moreland knew that this was another case where it didn't pay to judge a pony by its coat. He'd heard that the burly butcher, packing a trifle too much red-eye, had once shattered a man's jaw with one blow of a hamlike fist in a sudden spat of anger.

"Howdy, Al!" he greeted, easing past the squeaky screen door and stepping into the shop.

"Howdy, Sam!" boomed Jarvis. He paused, meat cleaver in hand, and turned, wiping beads of sweat from his forehead with his dingy white apron. His broad features crinkled. "Guess you law hounds finally got yourselves a job, corralling that killer."

"Jim passed the chore to me," returned Moreland. "Right now I'm rounding up the evidence. This Heckel hombre trade talk with anyone after I left the saloon?"

"Nary a word," the butcher replied

promptly. "Guess he was an all-fired lone wolf. He swallowed a couple of shots and drifted outside."

"And you next lamped him when?"

"When I tripped over his boots," grinned Jarvis. "Guess I was packing a load myself. The gent was all spraddled out in the alley. I sprawled arse over tip. Ed Sanders give me a hand up, and says, 'Who in hell's this drunk?' He strikes a stinker and yells, 'The hairpin's deader'n a can of corned beef.' Then I hotfoot for the sheriff and Ed hits for your room."

"That's all you know?"

Jarvis regarded his interrogator good-humoredly. "What else could I know?"

"That Heckel was packing a dodger offering five hundred dollars for your arrest. Seems you're dodging a murder warrant, Al."

For an instant Moreland glimpsed raw anger flaming in the big butcher's mild eyes — swift as a lightning flash on a sultry day, and gone as fast. When the butcher spoke his voice was calm, though it had lost its jovial overtones. "They named it murder, Sam," he said mildly, "but I figure different. Them days I had a wife, pretty as a china doll. There was talk. One day I hit for home, early. A no good saddlebum was laying her in the bedroom. I slapped her down and grabbed the coyote." His tone deepened with emotion, almost choked in his throat. "Twisted his head till his neck snapped. Then I lit out. You call that murder? I call it justice!"

"You'd kill again to escape the noose!"

The burly butcher slowly shook his head. "Nope, Sam, I couldn't harm a fly."

"Except when you get a mad on! Wal, someone beefed Heckel."

"Not me! Heck, I got a witness."

"Sure," returned the deputy dryly. "Bigfoot Sanders. You two wouldn't have cooked this up between you?" Alert for trouble, he saw the fingers of the hand grasping the heavy cleaver tighten. But the butcher controlled himself with visible effort. "Sam," he said quietly, too quietly. "You better go!"

Without further word, the deputy turned and left. Jarvis, he reflected, didn't act like a guilty man. Sanders now, well, he'd swear the liveryman had something on his mind.

IX

Two of his four suspects remained, considered Moreland, when he left the butcher shop, but unless he could induce the sheriff to give him a little more time he'd never get around to them. Likely Robinson was already waiting over at the law shack. Might just as well get some chuck under his belt before he faced up to the old buffalo. Deep down he knew it was just an excuse, to postpone the meeting — and arrest.

When he entered the Good Eats several townsmen were bunched at the counter, talk buzzing between them. He slid onto a stool as far distant as possible; he just didn't feel in the mood for company. From snatches of talk that drifted to his ears he gathered the patrons were engrossed in but one subject — the murder. And the pert waitress wasn't missing a word.

He knuckled the counter to attract her attention and bawled out "Flapjacks and coffee!" when her head turned.

"Isn't it horrible!" she exclaimed, when she set a smoking stack of flapjacks before him. "Just like —" She broke off.

"Just like the bank manager at Cottonwood," put in Moreland starkly, "for which I drew life. Want to pin this one on me, too?"

The girl eyed him thoughtfully. "No," she confessed, "you certainly weren't the man I saw."

"Saw what — when?" he queried sharply.

"Just about midnight," she explained, "I opened the window to chase away a squawling cat. A man slipped out of the alley on the far side of the saloon and skulked away, past the rear of the general store."

"The body was found in that alley!" Moreland was all attention now.

She nodded. "It could have been the murderer, running away."

"Would you know him again?" inquired the deputy eagerly. A witness! This was a stroke of luck he'd never dreamed of. Then his spirits dropped when the waitress shook her head. "N-no," she admitted. "It was dark and cloudy. He seemed scarcely more than a shadow."

"Was the jasper short, tall, fat, thin?" probed the deputy.

"Not tall, like you," she decided.

"That could cover most any man in town," he returned, with a touch of irritation.

"It's the best I can do," she snapped. "After all, you're paid to catch criminals, not me."

"You're doing fine!" he soothed. If her testimony didn't pin down the killer, he thought, at least it would help clear him.

When he reported at the law shack, the sheriff was seated at the table, chewing on his pipe stem and placidly shuffling through the stack of dodgers that had been left by

Moreland. If Robinson was surprised to find him still around, reflected the deputy, it didn't show.

"Wal?" he grunted.

"I'm sticking around," said Moreland. "I've got four suspects and found a witness who'll clear me."

"Yeah?"

He told of the waitress who had seen a man dart out of the alley around midnight. "And not tall, like me," he concluded. "The gal will swear to that."

"Is that the best she can do?" Robinson wanted to know, with quickening interest.

"Yep!" Moreland told him. "It was cloudy and not more than a sliver of moon. She claims he wasn't much more than a shadow."

"The suspects?" prompted Robinson.

Moreland pulled the four wanted dodgers from a pants pocket and tossed them onto the table. "Al Jarvis, Bigfoot Sanders, Baldy the barkeep and Jonathan Whitestone. I lamped 'em all in the Wagon Wheel afore the killing and three are wanted for murder. Whitestone's dodging a Yuma County warrant for embezzlement and juggling a mining company's books." He nodded at the dodgers he had left on the table. "There may be more." Then he remembered the rider on the piebald. "I picked up another lead, too."

In response to Robinson's questioning glance, he told of the man who had slid out of the livery at dawn, forking a piebald pony, and Sanders' emphatic denial that either horse or man existed. "Bigfoot's covering for the jasper," he concluded.

"Why in thunder didn't you take after him?" demanded Robinson.

"Guess I just didn't think fast enough," confessed the deputy ruefully. "Reckon my conk was kinda muddled after digging into dodgers all night." Mentally, he cursed himself for a hammerhead. Any man who had the brains of a bumblebee, he thought, would have hit the trail of that elusive stranger. Odds were he was the killer. While the fugitive was busily engaged in putting distance between himself and Mustang, he, Sam Moreland, had been frittering away time. He sure was not cut out to be a lawman. From the annoyance reflected in Robinson's eyes, he guessed the sheriff knew it. Lamely, he added, "I figure to get after the gent and stick to his trail till I get saddlesores. That is" — his tone became belligerent — "ef you're willing to give me more time."

"You got all the time in the world, Sam,"

returned the sheriff blandly. At least, thought his deputy, with relief, there was no more talk of handcuffs.

The ironshod hooves of Moreland's black clattered on the planks of the bridge that spanned Cold Creek, following a trail that led westward.

Moreland felt his spirits rising as the miles dropped behind. His pulse speeded with the exhilaration of action, after days of listless sitting around Mustang. He would have thoroughly enjoyed the *pasear* but for the killing that weighed on his mind — until the guilty man was run down, he knew he would be suspect in the sheriff's mind.

There is a popular misconception that a fugitive will find the most secure refuge by seeking the isolation of the lonely places — heading into wild terrain or burying himself deep in the barren breaks that know little life beyond soaring eagles and questing cougars. There is no greater fallacy. Where there are few men, the presence of a stranger is more likely to be marked. In crowded cities a man may pass unnoticed, an insignificant unit in the surging pack of humanity. In the lonely places an intruder is always conspicuous. Ragged prospectors note his passing; isolated homesteaders speculate upon his business; solitary sheepherders, wolf hunters, trailwise punchers knifing into the solitudes to round up strays, mark his meanderings. He betrays his presence by the tracks of his mount, the glitter of a bright sun on his pony's rigging, the ashes of his fires. Engulfed by seeming loneliness, he is never alone. Every move is marked.

And, sooner or later, a yearning for sound of a human voice, or the necessity for supplies, will draw him to a friendly campfire or a settler's shack. In the solitudes there is no place to hide.

Born and raised on the range, Moreland knew these things. It made sense that the fugitive would stick to the hill country, seeking security in its tangle of ravines and canyons. Circulate long enough among men who made the wilds their habitation, he reasoned, and he'd pick up a clue to the whereabouts of the rider straddling a piebald pony. In a country where five mounts out of six were duns or bays, that piebald would stick out like a sore thumb. It was just a question of time and patience. He had both.

Chewing over the killing as his mount jogged along the trail, one question bothered him. Why had the killer waited for daybreak before hightailing? The suspect's dawdling presented a factor that he just didn't understand.

The terrain began to smooth out, undulating into swelling, smooth-topped hills. A finger of smoke wavered skyward, coiling above the shoulder of a ridge. Moreland angled toward it, threading between slopes crusted with squat brush. In a shady draw dotted with scrub oak he pulled up outside a rude log hut. Scrawny hens pecked around discarded cans and bottles scattered over the ground; several scrub yearlings were confined in a pole corral and a spur-scratched dun was secured by a rope macarty to a tree. It was a typical hardscrabble spread, one of dozens dotted through the hills, where men haunted by old crimes eked out a lonely existence, and blessed the sheriff of Culver County.

At Moreland's hail, a bearded man in patched denims came to the door of the shack and stood eyeing, without speaking, the metal badge pinned to the front of his visitor's shirt.

"Any strangers around lately?" inquired the deputy.

"Nope!" the bearded man told him forcefully.

"I'm looking for a gent forking a piebald."

"He sure ain't been around here." With

85

that, the squatter stepped back and slammed the door.

Moreland's lips quirked with annoyance. Seemed he was using the wrong approach. Wheeling away, he unhooked the metal badge and dropped it into a pocket.

Before noon he had made three more calls upon isolated settlers, ostensibly hunting an old pard who forked a piebald pony. But he drew a blank every time.

In no wise daunted, for he had yet to cover a wide spread of country, he drew rein beside a murmuring creek, shaded by low-spread willows. Slackening the black's cinches, he picketed the pony in thick-growing grass, punctured a can of tomato juice and hunkered beside a willow, sipping the juice and watching the clear water surging over a gravelly bed. When Moreland finished his juice, he built a cigarette and lingered there. Finally, he crushed a butt and regretfully rose — murders weren't solved by deputies who lazed beside creeks.

Again he began working westward — and hit pay dirt on his first call. The settler, a grizzled old-timer, probed him with shrewd eyes while he pitched a yarn of hunting Gus Farley, an old pard who had a yen for piebald ponies.

"You ain't no lawman?" queried the old-timer doubtfully.

"Me!" With a broad grin, Moreland dug out the dodger displaying his features and carrying his description. The other carefully looked it over, then volunteered, "Don't know no Farley, but Ted Larner, my neighbor, forks a piebald, deals in hosses, too."

"Could be Farley switched monikers," said Moreland. "Where'll I locate the gent?"

"Ted was around this forenoon, fresh from Mustang. Guess he's back at his place right now — ride west a mile or so, you'll strike Cow Crick. Follow it downstream till you reach the fork. Ted's place ain't a spit and a holler away."

"I'm sure thanking you, mister," said Moreland fervently. This Larner was plainly his man. Lady Luck sure was in a friendly mood.

X

Moreland headed back to the creek where he had nooned. When he hit it, he turned downstream, following a well-defined trail that bore traces of recent use. At the fork, the trail slanted away, curving through thick chaparral. Cautiously now, he eased his mount along it. Larner's place could not be far distant, and when a man was fresh from a killing it came easy to stage a repeat performance.

He checked the pony when the brush began to thin. Ahead lay a flat, botched with clumped mesquite. And on the flat, not half a mile distant, stood a frame cabin with the usual shanty barn nearby. Drifting around a pasture enclosed by a three-strand barbed wire fence, he counted five ponies, among them a piebald.

His pulse speeded with excitement. The old-timer had steered him right. This must be the killer's place: he had just ridden out from Mustang, he forked a piebald pony.

The cabin seemed deserted. No smoke issued from its stovepipe chimney; there was no sign of life around it.

Thoughtfully, he sat the saddle, eyeing the flat stretch of terrain between himself and the cabin. Likely, he reflected, Larner was jittery and wary of pursuit. The suspect could blast him out of the saddle with a rifle before he was halfway across that flat. Wheeling, he pulled back to the concealment of heavier brush, looped his reins around the slender trunk of an aspen and pinned on his badge. Then he headed back, afoot.

Crouched, he began moving in, zigzagging across the flat as he dodged from the cover of one mesquite clump to another. Fifty paces or so from his goal, he paused behind a bushy mesquite and carefully surveyed the cabin. The place still seemed deserted. If it weren't for the fact that Larner's saddle horse had been turned out to pasture and his saddle lay by the pole gate, Moreland would have sworn that the quarry had fled. Debating his next move, he crouched, eyeing the grazing ponies with the appreciation of a man who knew good horseflesh. The hombre sure handled prime stock, he reflected; every one was high-grade. Then he forgot horses as a man's form filled the cabin doorway.

Casually building a cigarette, the stranger looked around, touched a match to the smoke and dropped carelessly onto a bench that fronted the cabin.

Moreland weighed him through a tracery of branches. He was sparely-built, with thin, weathered features. A drooping moustache hid his mouth and a battered felt hat was set upon a tangle of dark hair. He was garbed in a faded blue shirt, dirt-grimed Levi's and high boots. A gunbelt sagged around his lean waist.

A tough hombre, considered the deputy, and his sudden appearance had effectually pinned him — Moreland — down. The moment he left the cover of the mesquite he would be in plain view. True, he could gamble on matching cutters, but his job was to capture a killer, not provoke a gunfight.

The man he was watching abruptly ended his predicament by rising and sauntering toward the well in the middle of the yard. Now he was turned away, his back toward Moreland. Eager to grasp the opportunity, the deputy quickly shucked his spurs. Jerking his gun, he emerged from cover and began easing toward the cabin, eyes focused upon his quarry. Unsuspecting, Larner had lifted the bucket, was priming the pump. The clanking effectively smothered sound of the fast-moving deputy's approach. Moreland passed the cabin and, now not more than twenty paces distant, slowed to a walk and moved up behind Larner. Suddenly, quick as a startled cat, Larner spun around — to face a leveled gun.

Hard and belligerent, his glance flicked from the .45 to the law badge.

"You packing a warrant?" he grated.

"Nope!" said Moreland.

"Then why in hell are you holding a gun on me?"

"For the murder of Mike Heckel."

"Mike — who?"

"Heckel."

Larner's sun-blackened features registered frowning perplexity. "Never met the hombre," he declared.

"Quit horsing around," growled Moreland. "Heckel was throttled in Mustang last night. You were skulking around. I got you pegged for the killer."

The hardcase laughed out loud. "Hell, mister," he said tolerantly, "I got you placed now. You're Robinson's raw deputy. Wal, you tangled your spurs. Why in thunder would I beef this Heckel hombre?"

"Maybe he was packing the warrant you're dodging."

Larner raised his thin shoulders with a gesture of resignation, as though he knew further argument was futile.

"Unbuckle that gunbelt, easy-like, and let it drop," directed Moreland tautly, striving to keep the pride of his first arrest out of his voice.

In no haste, Larner slipped the buckle of his gunbelt. It thudded to the ground, lay curved around his feet. "Listen," he pleaded, as the deputy edged cautiously toward him. "Can't we chew this over? I had business in Mustang with Bigfoot Sanders. He'll testify I never left the livery. What's more, I rode in after the killing."

"So you were wise that Heckel was killed?"

"Sure, Bigfoot was busting with the news."

"I guess, Larner, you better save your arguing for the sheriff," decided Moreland. "To me, the finger points straight at you."

The sun was setting when they rode in — a resigned hardcase forking a piebald, and a jubilant young deputy jogging beside him, his prisoner's gunbelt hitched on the saddle horn.

Moreland headed straight for the livery. He was convinced that Larner and Bigfoot were working in cahoots and he craved to haul both before Sheriff Robinson.

Dismounting in the runway of the big barn, he escorted Larner to the door of Sanders' cubbyhole, a gun nudging the prisoner's back. Reaching with his free hand, he threw the door open — and stiffened with surprise when he saw the sheriff, hunched on a straightback chair, stolidly smoking, while the liveryman perched on the truckle bed, unshaved jaw working on a chaw.

"Wal," Moreland announced, "I got the killer!"

"A lowdown hyena!" agreed Sanders, and Moreland saw amusement flicker in his shifty eyes.

"And I figure you're tied in, too," threw

back the deputy shortly, and transferred his attention to the sheriff. "The hairpin was forking the piebald," he told Robinson, and pushed Larner forward. "He admits he was in town."

"You don't say!" returned the sheriff imperturbably.

Larner grinned crookedly at Sanders and mutely lifted his shoulders. The sheriff continued to draw on his briar.

"Bigfoot's got some explaining to do, too," added Moreland.

"Wise him up, Bigfoot," said the sheriff, a trace of impatience on his tone.

The liveryman's wizened features creased into a grin. "It's like this, Sam," he explained with relish. "Me and Ted here been doing business for years. He peddles hosses, I buy 'em. Last night, after the killing, he ambles in with two duns and a buckskin, beds down on the straw pile back of the barn like he always does, and pulls out at sunup."

Moreland considered this, puzzled glance shuttling from Sanders to the sheriff. "So why'd you deny it?" he inquired tautly of Bigfoot.

"Stolen horses," explained Robinson patiently, and added quickly, "stolen outside the county."

"And you were wise?" Moreland eyed his superior with slack-jawed amazement.

Robinson nodded.

"It's against the law!"

"In Culver County I make the law," said the sheriff stiffly. "Live and let live!" He heaved to his feet and moved toward the door; on the threshold he paused and swung around. His granite-gray eyes focused on Larner. "You got till sundown to get out of the county," he said shortly. "Stealing horses outside my bailiwick is none of my business, but tipping your hand is." With that, he trudged away.

Battling bewilderment, the deputy holstered his gun. Sanders and Larner stood eyeing each other, dejection reflected on their weathered features. Robinson, considered the chagrined Moreland, sure had flexible ideas on what constituted crime. Glumly, he turned to leave. Larner's grating voice halted him, his tone tinged with caustic amusement. "You tried, mister, but ef I'd downed this Heckel I'd have tagged yuh afore we left Cow Creek." He bent, dipped into the top of a riding boot and lifted out a squat derringer. "Mebbe I would have bedded you down anyway," he continued thoughtfully, "but I figured Robinson would have run me out of the county." His thin lips twisted. "Seems he's running me out anyways."

XI

Stung by Larner's derisive revelation, Moreland left the livery. A jackass, he thought glumly, would make a better lawman.

That evening he just couldn't bring himself to face the citizens of Mustang, even to eat supper in Ed Sayers' restaurant. Bigfoot would have spread the story of the hidden derringer all over. He could imagine the derision with which calloused townsmen would eye him.

Hunger, however, is hard to ignore, particularly by a young and healthy man. Next morning he overcame his qualms and headed for the Good Eats. A smattering of townsmen were eating and he sensed, not amusement, but cold hostility in their quick side glances. Usually, Ed Sayers' patrons were a friendly bunch, always ready to trade talk. Today every man ate in chilly silence. The reason was plain to Moreland: Mustang had reached a verdict and decided that its new deputy was Heckel's killer, likely because he was one of the wanted men the bounty hunter was stalking. Likely they didn't give a hoot whether Heckel lived or died, reflected the deputy, eating amid a quiet disturbed only by the rattle of knives and forks. It was the manner of the killing that nauseated them. A gunshot wound might be bloody but it was clean; a strangling turned any man's stomach.

When he legged across to the law shack, he was conscious of the same frigid atmosphere. True, the sheriff said nothing, just lumped as usual on a chair tilted against the front of the shack, silently puffing his pipe, but Moreland read condemnation in his gray eyes. And the deputy's "Howdy!" evoked only a grunt.

It was apparent that his company wasn't welcome, so he wandered inside the office and killed time examining and reexamining the balance of the wanted dodgers abstracted from Heckel's saddlebag, seeking fruitlessly to uncover a clue that would give him some indication of the killer.

The notion that he had beefed the stranger seemed to have percolated all over town, he mused gloomily. That would likely be Bigfoot Sanders' doing. He had busted up the liveryman's profitable horse-trading deal. Anyway, Bigfoot had been hostile from the start.

Chewing a cold butt, he rehashed the killing in his mind. He had yet to brace two of his four suspects, but he had a hunch it would be time wasted. Baldy had been tied down at the bar, and Whitestone just didn't have the earmarks of a killer. It was doubtful if the embezzler'd even have strength enough to overcome a tough hombre like Heckel.

That left him where he'd started — plumb up against a blank wall.

Remembrance of one unexplained detail drifted into his mind — the initials "B.O." done in brass studs on the dead man's saddle. Heckel's initials would be "M.H." Likely the variance meant nothing. Heckel might have won the kak in a poker game, or bought it from some puncher down on his uppers.

Moreland rose and stood staring gloomily out of a window. Robinson's chair outside had emptied. Usually the sheriff told him where he was likely to be found when he left the office, but this time he'd omitted the courtesy. Another sign of waning confidence, thought the deputy.

Two small boys, yelling, raised dust across the square; other children were straying from the direction of the schoolhouse, which reminded the troubled Moreland of the schoolma'am. It had become routine to meet her after school and walk her home.

Due to the killing, he'd failed to show for the past two days.

It was hard to figure the fascinating Phyllis Robinson, he pondered. She was friendly, but no more. Sometimes he had the impression that she tolerated him just because she liked to have a man at her beck and call. The girl was pretty as a heart flush and cold as a chunk of ice. She had only to crook a finger and men came arunning, but the women wanted none of her — a sentiment which the haughty sheriff's daughter heartily reciprocated. He fell to comparing her in his mind with the outspoken Mildred Hogan, the waitress with the pert nose and freckles. Phyllis sure had the Hogan girl shaded where looks were concerned, and she was as smooth as silk, but a man knew where he stood with the waitress. Like, she figured him lower than a snake's belly, convinced that he'd garroted the Cottonwood banker, and he knew it.

He blinked. As though his thoughts had summoned her, the schoolma'am was walking toward the law shack, moving unhurriedly, with languid grace.

He went to the doorway, called, "Howdy!"

She looked him over, coolly and casually. "Hello, Sam, I thought you'd deserted me."

"Heckel's killing kept me hustling." His tone was apologetic.

"As a matter of fact," she said, "that's what brought me over. Isn't it time you quit this playacting?"

The deputy eyed her, brow creased with perplexity. "Playacting?" he echoed.

"Everyone knows you killed Heckel," she stated calmly.

He stood numb, too flabbergasted to speak.

Her lips curled with amusement. "Perhaps I'm too outspoken. To be frank, the affair doesn't particularly shock me, killers are so common in Culver County. The whole town is convinced that you — choked — this Heckel person. Weren't you convicted of a similar crime in Texas?"

Moreland stood frowning angrily, knowing the futility of argument. After a pause, he came back tightly, "The evidence of Milly Hogan, waitress in the Good Eats, clears me of this killing."

"Who would accept the word of a kitchen slut?" she retorted contemptuously. "Anyway, all she claims to have seen is a shadow."

Mrs. Larcombe was right, he thought, Robinson's queenly daughter was a stuck-up, self-opinionated piece of baggage, with an acid tongue; he'd been crazy to chase after her. Aloud, he said curtly, "Milly's no slut!"

"Use your own expression!" she countered with a shrug. "Her testimony certainly won't help you cheat the hangman."

"Dammit, I'm clean!"

The girl ignored his protest. "I like you, Sam," she said earnestly; "that's why I'm here. I can understand your predicament. Heckel was hunting you — you ended his life. You were realistic, why not be realistic now? Folks think you're guilty. Sooner or later, Dad will be compelled to take action. This is the first homicide in the county since he became sheriff. Do you think he welcomes the embarrassment of placing his own deputy on trial?" Her voice deepened with pleading. "Leave! That will solve the problem and save your own neck."

"I light out, I'm confessing guilt."

She sighed. "Do you think you're fooling anyone now? When you leave, the whole wretched business will be forgotten. Don't you think you owe something to Dad, and to me?"

She came to her feet, caressed his shirted arm with slim fingers. "Believe me, Sam," she urged softly, "it's the best way." She pressed his arm and moved away. Unhurriedly, she stepped through the doorway, sauntered across the square.

Alone, Moreland paced the office, grappling with a confusion of thought. He should thank Phyllis Robinson, he told himself. Like most everyone else, she figured him guilty. But she thought enough of him to advise him to leave before the inevitable moment of arrest arrived. Odds were, the sheriff had confided in her that he shrank from the notoriety of a trial. The old warthog was proud of his county's record. If his deputy made himself scarce, the whole problem would be solved. As the girl said, memory of the killing would soon fade. A murder didn't make too much impression on Culver County's calloused citizens.

Seemed he was through in Mustang, anyway. Even if the sheriff didn't charge him, or lift his badge, he was condemned in the public eye. He'd be fighting a lonely battle, with no chance of victory. It made good sense to hightail and shuck the whole mess.

Then, with a muttered oath, he checked and crushed a cold cigarette beneath a boot toe. Somewhere around Mustang the real killer was watching and enjoying all this, gleefully chewing on the fact that he'd gotten away with murder. Odds were he was a former member of the Garrote Gang. He,

Sam Moreland, had ridden west to dig out the gang. Now he had evidence that at least one was around, and he was riding away. Maybe he had turned out to be a lousy deputy but he'd be damned if he'd quit.

XII

Moreland didn't see the sheriff again before morning. When he legged over to the office, after feeding his tapeworm, Robinson was lumped in his tilted chair, impassively eyeing the sluggish life of Mustang stirring beyond the square.

"Jim," announced the deputy, striding up, "I'm heading for Lennox."

"Lennox!" The sheriff's eyebrows raised.

"I just got to get a line on Heckel's killer. Most hombres heading for Mustang lay over in Lennox — ain't no other settlement within a day's ride. Maybe I can pick up something there."

"Maybe," agreed Robinson dryly.

"Guess I'll throw my stuff together and light out — pronto."

"A right good idea," approved the sheriff.

Moreland didn't have to guess. He knew from the tone of Robinson's voice that the sheriff figured he was making a getaway, and that nothing he could say would convince the lawman otherwise. Odds were, the sheriff had sicced his attractive daughter onto him, well knowing a good-looking girl could be more persuasive than any man. So, without further word, he swung on a heel and headed for the hotel to get his gear.

As a crow flies, Lennox lay twenty-three miles northwest of Mustang, but the lone trail that linked the two county-seats ribboned over thirty-four miles of rugged terrain. When Moreland's pony stirred the dust of Lennox's broad Main Street night was closing in. Saddlesore and dust-grayed, the deputy wheeled to a water trough and allowed the hock-scarred black a drink. Then he added his mount to a row of saddle horses lazily switching tails along a saloon hitch-post. Easing stiff limbs, he stood eyeing the darkening street. Compared to Mustang, he decided, Lennox was a metropolis, boasting a bank, land office, courthouse, two hotels, a church, not to mention three saloons. Vague in the fading light, punchers drifted into town, stirring lazy dust; a string of ponderous freight wagons ground past, the big Murphys jolting over the potholes behind strings of mules; knots of men loitered beneath the wooden awnings of garish-lit saloons; saddle horses stood thick along the hitchrails; the tinny music of a piano mingled with the pistol-like cracking of teamsters' whips. With sundown, as the heat of the plains abated, Lennox was crawling with activity.

His survey complete, Moreland ducked under the rail and pushed into the saloon for a quick shot of bourbon to wash the trail dust out of his throat. Emerging, he loosed the black and stepped into the saddle again, drifting down the street toward the court-house.

Plugging up the red-bricked courthouse steps, he reflected he knew nothing of Sheriff Lanker beyond that the Lennox County sheriff was reputed to be a salty hombre who enforced the statutes from A to Z. Seeing that he hailed from Culver County, thought the deputy whimsically, odds were that Lanker would throw him out as fast as a saloon bouncer ejected a trouble-some drunk.

He pushed through the swinging doors into a wide corridor, faintly lit by lamps bracketed on the walls. He moved down the corridor, scanning neatly lettered inscrip-tions on doors. The last door to the right bore the emblem: JOSEPH LANKER, SHER-IFF.

He turned the handle, stepped inside and

found himself in a high-ceilinged room, divided in half by a low, polished wood railing with a swinging gate. The side of the railing upon which he stood was bare except for several straightback chairs and neat rows of wanted dodgers tacked on the far wall. Two of the chairs were occupied by tough-looking deputies, puffing smokes and trading talk.

Beyond the railing, he focused on the gray-shirted back of a bony man with thinning hair, seated at a scratched rolltop desk. The dome of his head was bald as a brown eggshell. A gunbelt and shapeless old Stetson hung from pegs within reach.

One of the deputies glanced up, eyed the metal badge pinned to Moreland's shirt front and drawled, "What's on your mind, pard?"

"Sheriff Lanker," said Moreland.

"Joe!" bawled the deputy, "you got company."

The lawman at the desk spun around in his swivel chair. A tough old moseyhorn, registered Moreland, eyeing the sheriff's long, deadpan features, over which the skin, tanned to the hue of mahogany, was stretched drum-tight. A fringe of moustache drooped over uncompromising lips, and there was the glint of steel in the appraising glance he directed toward his visitor.

"The moniker's Moreland," volunteered the deputy. "I crave a word with you."

"Wal, step in and rest your legs," drawled Lanker, indicating a nearby chair.

Moreland pushed back the gate and dropped down on the chair. "Deputy, Sheriff Robinson's office, Mustang," he volunteered, as Lanker's glance dropped to his badge.

"They got law in Culver County?" inquired the sheriff in dry, nasal tones.

"Of a sort!" returned Moreland, forcing a smile. "I'm hunting a killer."

"You sure got a fistful in your own backyard."

"And no need for a jail," returned Moreland brittlely.

Lanker's mahogany features creased into the parody of a grin. "Maybe so. Now about this killer?"

As Moreland began to relate the story of the bounty hunter's visit and his sudden demise, the sheriff lifted a sack of tobacco from a pocket of his dangling vest and built a cigarette, his faded eyes never leaving the visitor's face.

"So this Heckel hombre was throttled, likely by the jasper he was trailing," he commented, when Moreland was through.

"Why brace me?"

The deputy hesitated. "This is kinda personal," he confessed. "Folks got me tagged for the killing — we tangled in the saloon an hour or two before he was beefed. I came up with nothing around Mustang," explained Moreland, "and rode down on a gamble. Figured maybe you might be acquainted with this Heckel gent and I'd pick up a lead."

"Never heard of the hairpin," declared Lanker.

Moreland stifled rising disappointment, forced a grin. "Wal, I guess it was a crazy notion," he admitted. "There was just a long chance Heckel might have tangled with some hombre in Lennox. The jasper coulda dogged him to Mustang and put out his light."

"Strangled!" murmured Lanker. "A queer way to kill. Reminds me of the Garrote Gang, back in Texas."

XIII

Now he had no option but to sit and listen while a garrulous old-timer resurrected past memories, thought Moreland resignedly. He couldn't walk out on the old coot.

"Is that so?" he prompted, and assumed

an attitude of respectful attention.

"Worse pack of wolves ever to plague the state," mused Lanker, settling more comfortably in his chair. "There was four of the lobos, specialized in bank heists, and they sure had a method all their own. Trouble was, not one of their maps ever decorated a dodger."

"How come?" interjected Moreland, to register interest. As if he didn't know, he thought.

"They never left a witness alive; garroted the poor bustards."

Moreland made a smoke and wondered how long the recital would drag out.

"I was deputy at Myberg," droned on Lanker. "One time I staked out our bank night after night, for weeks, figuring that ef you set in a poker game long enough you'll draw an ace. And damned ef I didn't!

"One night I'm hunkered under the canopy of the Martell Saddlery, across the street from the bank, nursing a Winchester and needing toothpicks to prop my eyelids up, when four riders drift down the street. One pony carried double. Right then I knew I'd hit the jackpot and snap wide awake. The hombres pull to the rail and peel out of leather. Three head for the bank door, yanking a prisoner along. The fourth holds the hosses. Trouble was that the moon was quartering and clouded up, so the light was bad and they wasn't much more'n shadows. I'm so excited the Winchester slips. The clatter's a clean giveaway. By the time I grab up the gun and lever, the sidewinders panic. All I could lamp was a blur of bodies — rising dust when they hit leather blots 'em out altogether. I head for the bank and damned ef I don't trip over an hombre squirming on the street. I'd tagged one of the sidewinders and he was flopping around, his right leg smashed by the slug. The bank manager's sprawled by the hitchrail — they'd found time to garrote the poor bustard.

"The governor," concluded Lanker complacently, "give me a fancy rifle and I was a shoo-in for sheriff at the next election."

"And that was the end of the Garrote Gang," contributed Moreland, repressing a yawn. He knew it all.

"Sure, Buckskin O'Brien, the hombre I tagged, spilled his guts to dodge the rope. Seemed Buckskin was a deserter from the Twelfth Cavalry. He gave good descriptions of his pards, swore their leader, Dutch, handled the garroting. But the coyotes were never corralled. Guess they split up, mebbe ducked across the border."

Some half-buried memory itched in Moreland's mind, but he couldn't pin it down. Then, in a flash, it became plain — B.O. Those were the initials marked with brass studs on Heckel's saddle. And the murdered man rode like a cavalryman and walked stiff-legged, as though from an old wound.

Pulse speeding with the excitement of discovery, he inquired eagerly, "This O'Brien! He spare-built, long jaw, dark hair, walk with a limp?"

"Sure! You acquainted with the sidewinder?"

"That was the gent who called himself Heckel, the hombre who was throttled. His saddle carried the initials 'B.O.' "

"I'll be doggoned!" Lanker made another smoke, pondering on this. "It would be five years since Buckskin was sent down," he mused. "Guess he served his term."

"And turned bounty hunter."

"Could be," ruminated the sheriff. "Likely Buckskin run across a member of the old gang in Mustang — you got a choice assortment of rattlers up there — and the hairpin paid him off for ratting on the bunch at Myberg."

"Or maybe he was trailing 'em," threw back Moreland. "I heard talk, back in Texas, that he was almighty sore because his pards quit him and he never got a cut of the kitty.

This sure begins to add up." The deputy was conscious of rising elation. Finally, light had begun to glimmer through the fog of mystery that enveloped the Heckel killing. By sheer chance he had uncovered a motive. What was more, it placed one or more members of the Garrote Gang in Mustang. Now he *had* to uncover the killer.

"Where would I get hold of dodgers describing this Garrote bunch?" he inquired.

"Damned ef I know," acknowledged Lanker. "The gang's most forgotten now, ain't much more'n a memory. Guess there just ain't any of the old dodgers around."

"You wouldn't recollect the descriptions?"

"Hell!" The sheriff smiled tolerantly. "Must be years since that gang busted up." He gestured toward the display of dodgers arrayed on the wall. "I've lamped scores, hundreds, of dodgers since. You expect a man to remember?"

"Guess not." Moreland hid his chagrin. He came to his feet, extended a hand. "It's sure been a pleasure meeting you, Sheriff, and a million thanks for the Garrote Gang lead."

"So the time wasn't altogether wasted listening to an old pelican's babbling," returned Lanker dryly.

Moreland's grin was twisted. "Sheriff," he said earnestly. "Your 'babbling' likely saved my badge, and could be my neck."

He rode back to Mustang in a far better frame of mind than that he had left with. At last he had something concrete to work on. If only he could get his hands on the dodgers describing the Garrote Gang, he thought, he could likely solve the mystery of Heckel's killing in quick time. But odds were all those old dodgers had been destroyed, years back. No sheriff would have reason to retain a dodger for five years or more. Even if he did, it would be faded, unreadable. His enthusiasm slowly evaporated as realization sank in that he was not much further ahead than he was before. Until he could identify the three fugitive members of the Garrote Gang he would still be groping in the dark.

To escape the blasting heat of the plains, he had pulled out of Lennox before sunup and it was still light when the black drummed across the plank bridge into Mustang.

Threading through an alley between two stores, he came in sight of the square, and quickened with surprise.

Hatless, a big, gaunt, rawboned fellow

with a black bushy beard and a wild mane of raven hair was declaiming on the bare stretch of ground. His shabby pants were secured around his waist by a strip of rawhide, the bottom thrust into cracked high boots. In the crook of one arm bulged a heavy, black-covered book. Strangest of all, he wore an ill-fitting frock coat, its dangling tails jerking in tune with his gestures. And, beneath the dragging frock coat, Moreland glimpsed a heavy gunbelt.

Piercing dark eyes, set like twin daggers in the stranger's desert-tanned features, sparked with fervor above a great beak of a nose, as he harangued a smattering of curious citizens lounging around him. His roaring denunciation poured into Moreland's ears: "Pause, ye unbelievers, teetering on the brink of Hell, pause and give thought to glorious salvation. Drop on your knees, prostrate yourselves, sinners, and thank the good Lord that Paul the Preacher has been moved to visit this ungodly county and salvage your wretched souls. Meditate upon your manifold sins, make peace with the Lord before He casts you into the blazing fires of eternal Hell." He held the black volume high. "The Good Book says, 'Repent and your sins shall be forgiven.' Who will be the first to repent and sit among the legions of bright angels beside the Golden Throne?"

He paused, mopping his brow with a red bandana. No one moved, and he launched upon another thundering denunciation: "So you would wallow in your wickedness, foul blotches upon the fair face of Creation! I perceive I labor upon stony ground. But Paul the Preacher is no quitter. Mark that, disbelievers! Mustang, this sink of iniquity, hath need of the Word. The Good Book says —"

Moreland never heard what the Good Book had to say on the subject, for he had rounded the preacher and his somewhat derisive audience and was heading for the law shack, outside of which the sheriff's blocky form was visible, hunched as usual on his tilted chair. It would take more than an itinerant preacher to lure Jim Robinson out of that chair, reflected Moreland.

He read surprise in the sheriff's eyes when he stepped out of the saddle, but Robinson made no comment, just inclined his head briefly and sat poker-faced.

"Jim," said the deputy, "Joe Lanker gave me a lead."

"Such as?" There was an ironical note in the sheriff's voice.

" 'Member the Garrote Gang?"

"I met one member," returned Robinson

114

pointedly.

Moreland ignored the crack. "Heckel was likely Buckskin O'Brien. He rode with the gang, was captured and sent down for five years. His time's up. He turns bounty hunter and drifts into town. I'm gambling there's one or two members of the gang skulking around. They remember he spilled his guts to the law, busted up the bunch, back in Texas."

"So?"

"Hell, they garroted the hombre."

"Quit hurrahin' me!" Lurking impatience roughened the sheriff's tone. "Heckel was hunting you."

"And a fistful of other fugitives."

"Wal, you rode with the gang — round up your suspects."

"Dammit, quit prodding me!" exploded the deputy. "Like I told you, I was framed. I wouldn't know the lobos from Adam."

Silently, the sheriff's bullet-gray eyes weighed him. "Yeah!" said Robinson caustically, and the deputy guessed he was far from convinced. But Moreland persisted, knowing that the only way he could convince the sheriff was by uncovering the real killer. "If we could locate them old dodgers, describing the Garrote bunch, we'd likely nail the garroter — and clear me."

Robinson knocked out his pipe, and refilled the bowl, considering this. "Doubt if any of them dodgers are around," he returned finally. "What's more, they wouldn't circulate outside of Texas."

"I gamble we could locate a set, if we dug hard enough," insisted Moreland.

The sheriff said nothing, puffing stolidly on his pipe.

"You got any connections in Texas?" prompted the deputy. "Phyllis claimed you packed a Cattle Association badge back there."

"Some," admitted Robinson.

"You'll get in touch?"

"When I'm convinced you're not running a blazer."

Moreland tautened with frustration. "I've a mind to ride back and poke around myself," he said.

"You forgot Huntsville?" inquired Robinson dryly.

Fuming with anger, and unable to do anything about it, Moreland led his mount to the shanty barn behind the shack and stripped off its gear.

In no good humor, he headed next for the eating house. When he brushed aside the fly curtain and dropped onto a stool to eat his supper, it was evident that the hostility that

116

had been so marked a few days before had evaporated. The shock of Heckel's killing was apparently wearing off. No one paid him any attention, but talk continued unabated and one or two careless nods were thrown his way.

Supper beneath his belt, he felt in a more amiable mood and sauntered back to the hotel. Mrs. Larcombe bulked behind the showcase.

"Wal, Ma," he greeted, grinning. "I'm back!"

"You showed more sense than I'd hoped for," she returned tartly. "Now we got a crazy preacher in town to plague us."

"Don't tell me he ain't needed."

"Them as need him never listen! Your room's ready — clean sheets and a new counterpane." She reached, lifted a key off the rack and tossed it to him.

He jingled down the passageway to his room, unlocked the door. Stepping inside, he hooked his Stetson on a peg. Beams of the setting sun, streaming through the open window, made a broad shaft of light that splashed over the bed. But his gaze was attracted, not by the crisp new counterpane that covered it, but by a rawhide lace, neatly arranged in its center. The slender thong was tied in the shape of a hangman's noose, and the implication was plain. Brow creased, Moreland picked it up. It might mean nothing more than a crude joke, he considered, but it might, too, be a grisly warning.

XIV

Just how had the intruder who left the gruesome token entered the room? wondered Moreland — no one could have gotten by Mrs. Larcombe in the lobby. Which meant that whoever had placed the noose on the bed had come in through the window. Drifting over to the open window, he stood gazing out — and down. It was not a four-foot drop from the windowsill to the ground. Sliding the window higher, he cocked a leg over the sill and dropped down. Turning carefully in his own tracks, he stood scrutinizing the sandy ground. Imprints of boots were plain — oversize boots. There was only one man in town they would fit, he decided: Bigfoot Sanders. So Bigfoot either possessed a sense of humor, which he doubted, or the liveryman had good reason for trying to scare him away. What better reason than the fear that the real killer of Heckel would be uncovered?

He climbed back into the room, dropped the cord noose into a vest pocket and jammed on his hat.

When he pushed through the batwings of the Wagon Wheel it was still too early for serious drinking to get started. No more than a handful of patrons nursed drinks at the tables. At his gesture, Baldy, the apron, followed him down to the far end of the bar, out of earshot of the drinkers.

Baldy waddled up, stood mechanically swiping off the bar with a damp rag while waiting for the deputy to speak.

" 'Member the night Heckel was here?" inquired Moreland.

"Am I likely to forget it?" countered the barkeep dolefully.

"As I recollect," continued the deputy, "Bigfoot Sanders and Al Jarvis were bellied up to the bar. Did either, or anyone else, follow Heckel when he left?"

Baldy thumbed his chin. "Not right away," he decided. "Three or four of the boys drifted out later."

"Bigfoot among them?"

"Nope!" declared the apron decisively. "Bigfoot stuck around with Jarvis fer an hour, maybe longer. They pulled out together."

Seemed as though he'd guessed wrong, reflected Moreland, but Bigfoot wasn't in the clear yet. No one knew at what hour

Heckel had died.

"Why don't you quit sweating over that lousy bounty hunter?" put in Baldy. "Who gives a damn who beefed him?"

"I do!" said Moreland. "You forgot the finger points at me?" He left the saloon and cut across a corner of the square, heading for the livery barn in the beginning dusk.

He rapped the door of Sanders' cubbyhole briskly, and entered. Vague in the gloom, he glimpsed Bigfoot, hunched on the truckle bed, hastily thrust a pint bottle beneath the blanket. Nose wrinkling at the variegated stench of spilled liquor, body odor and horses in the poky little room, he wondered why the sheriff hadn't given this unsavory character marching orders at the same time he'd told Larner to vamoose.

"Drowning thoughts of your misdeeds?" he inquired curtly.

Bigfoot drew the back of a grimy paw across his mouth. "Can the wisecracks," he growled. "What you want?"

"A little light," snapped Moreland. "I hate to talk in the dark."

Bigfoot hesitated, then rose and lumbered across to where a stable lamp hung from a nail. Lifting it down, he set it on the stove top, levered up the glass funnel and touched a match to the wick. Sickly light bloomed.

"Wal?" grunted the liveryman, turning.

Moreland brought out the miniature noose, held it up. "How come you left this in my room?"

Bigfoot's small eyes shifted uneasily, to the right and left, anywhere but in the deputy's direction. "The hairpin who claims it was me is a dogblasted liar," he protested.

"Hell, quit fiddlefooting!" barked Moreland. "You left tracks beneath that window as big as an elephant's."

"I was just — hurrahin' you," muttered the other.

"You weren't scared," taunted the deputy, "scared I was getting too close to Heckel's killer?"

"You can't pin that on me!" shrilled Bigfoot, in a sudden spat of fury. "I got an alibi — Al Jarvis."

"Yep, Al will swear that you two stuck closer than pups on a warm brick," cut in Moreland harshly, "but that murder warrant Heckel packed still sticks in my mind. . . . It names you." His voice hardened. "Chew on this, Bigfoot: in my mind, you're still on the list of suspects. Pester me again and I'll knock them buck teeth right down your throat." With that, he turned and left, glad to get out of the stinking cubbyhole.

Back in his hotel room, he fretted around,

irked by frustration. Maybe the lace noose was the liveryman's idea of a joke but he was unable to banish a conviction of Bigfoot's guilt. The hostler had something on his mind, he'd swear to that. What was itching him?

He yanked the four creased wanted dodgers describing his four suspects from a pants pocket and dumped down on the bed, eyeing them. Thoughtfully, he reread Bigfoot's dodger. That knifing had taken place four years before in Tucson, he cogitated. Maybe this Thomas Hall, the sheriff who had circulated the dodger, still held office in Tucson and was acquainted with Bigfoot's background.

Tucson was quite a trip, he reflected: first a thirty-four-mile ride down to Lennox to pick up an Overland stage, then another hundred miles or more plugging across the plains. It would eat up the best part of a week, maybe a wasted week, but any kind of action was preferable to setting around Mustang, an object of suspicion. He'd picked up a good lead from Sheriff Lanker. Could be he'd draw an ace in Tucson.

He tackled Robinson the next morning just as soon as the sheriff stumped down to the law shack. First he detailed his suspicions of Bigfoot and the incident of the thong noose, then Bigfoot's flight from a murder warrant and his own theory that the liveryman had been tied up with the Garrote Gang. Concluding, he stated his intention of heading for Tucson to check further.

Robinson, dumped onto a chair, poker-faced, heard him out, then inquired mildly, "Sam, ain't it time you quit chowsing around like the heel flies was after you?"

"We've got a killer on the loose," returned the deputy defensively. "And I don't fancy folks slapping a murder brand on me."

"Simmer down!" soothed the sheriff. "It'll hair over."

"But I'd still pack the scar," remonstrated Moreland. "I'm nominating Bigfoot as the strangler and I aim to gather proof."

"Which includes heading for Tucson — on a hunch?"

"I hit pay dirt at Lennox!"

"We could argue about that," countered the sheriff good-naturedly, "but I can't back this Tucson trip. You expect Culver County to dig up dinero so you can rampage over the whole Territory, letting off steam?"

"I'll pay my own way."

Robinson relit his pipe and sat eyeing his deputy resignedly. "You're chasing a mirage, Sam," he insisted, with quiet forcefulness. "Granting you're clean, you can't stick Bigfoot with the killing — you forgot that ironclad alibi?"

"He's a killer and a killer alibied him," persisted Moreland.

"Stubborn as a Missouri mule!" grunted the sheriff. "Wal, what do you expect to find in Tucson?"

"Evidence!"

"Hogwash!" exclaimed Robinson forcefully. He turned his broad back to Moreland, indicating the discussion was at an end.

Anxious to make himself scarce before the sheriff flatly ordered him to stick around Mustang, the deputy hit for the door, hurried around to the shanty barn in the rear. Wasting no time, he rigged his pony, swung into leather.

Swaying on its broad leather springs, the big red Concord rolled down the length of Congress Street, Tucson, its six-horse team stretched out at full gallop. Buffalo Brady, the whiskered driver, always fancied entering town in style. Nearing the shaded front of the Mission Hotel, the dust-smothered team slacked down. Buffalo steered them exactly in front of the hotel and jammed on the foot brake. With a jolt, the stage came to a stop amid a rattle of harness. Sam

Moreland stepped out behind two drummers in linen dusters.

He'd boarded the stage at Lennox and through the night and most of the morning had swallowed dust and endured the heavy vehicle's joggling and lurching as it crawled across a desolate expanse of semi-desert, relieved only by brief stops at lonely way stations to change teams.

Stiff-limbed, he paused to take stock of the sprawling aggregation of earth-colored adobes and square-fronted rock-and-adobe stores that lined the wide street. A scattering of *rebozoed* señoras and blanketed squaws mingled with straw-hatted peons and jingling punchers on the plankwalks, all drifting unhurriedly beneath the shade of wooden canopies projecting from the fronts of saloons and stores. Ponies drowsed at the hitchrails, and slow-moving freight wagons ground over the ruts like weary centipedes. A spirit of lassitude seemed to envelop the whole settlement.

Tucson sure didn't live up to its hell-raising reputation, reflected the deputy. Maybe it was the heat; it was hotter than the hearthstones of Hell.

Bone-weary from the jolting of the stage and limp from the heat, he booked a room at the hotel, yanked off his boots, gratefully stretched out on a sagging bed, and drifted off to sleep.

The muted roar of a six-gun awakened him. Bemused, he sat up. Darkness mantled the hotel room, through which a discord of sound flowed to his ears. Still drowsy, he padded in his socks to the window. Sleepy Congress Street was transformed — men thronged saloon fronts, silhouetted by glaring flares, and rambled, thick as flies, along the plankwalks; shadowed riders passed and repassed, their ponies' hooves stirring ever-hovering dust; the plaintive melody of guitars mingled with the boisterous yelling of drunks, the tinkle of broken glass, the steady drumming of boots on the wooden plankwalks, all punctuated at irregular intervals by the roar of a forty-five.

First appearances, decided Moreland, were deceptive. He spilled water from a pitcher into the washstand, dug his shaving tackle out of the carpetbag he had brought along, and stripped to the waist. After he'd shaved and sluiced off, he stepped outside into the turbulence of Congress Street.

Sheriff Hall's office offered no respite from the turmoil through which he had elbowed on the street. As he stepped over the threshold, two deputies thrust him aside, hauling in a yelling, cursing teamster, plainly crazed by rotgut. Another prisoner flopped on the floor, clumsily fending off attempts of a deputy to search him prior to booking. A third drunk sagged on a bench, dull-eyed, blood seeping over his mouth from a smashed nose and steadily dripping off his unshaven chin. Behind a desk at the end of the room, a big, smooth-faced man, a sheriff badge pinned to his dark shirt, sat patiently listening to the angry tirade of a blowsy woman, coarse features thick with makeup, short skirt displaying plump legs swathed in silk. As Moreland stood back against a wall, watching, the sheriff finally silenced the harridan and a cold-eyed gambler in sober black, standing beside her, began speaking in clipped, precise accents. Moreland gathered he was accusing the woman of theft.

As he stood absorbing the shrill protests of the woman, the babble of drunks, the curses of panting deputies, Moreland thought longingly of the quiet law shack in Mustang.

A deputy hustled the yammering woman away, the gambler left with chilly decorum and Moreland grabbed the opportunity to brace the sheriff.

Hall greeted him with the smile of resigned amiability that is the trademark of the elected official.

"You got a real salty town," commented Moreland, introducing himself.

"Kinda quiet right now," said Hall. He weighed his visitor with shrewd eyes and waved him to a chair. "Culver County," he mused. "Seems I've heard it named something different."

"Renegade Roost, or maybe Robbers' Roost," admitted Moreland, with a grin, "but we got law, of a sort." He pulled out the dodger that described Bigfoot. "What do you know about this hombre?"

Hall eyed the dog-eared sheet, decorated with Sanders', alias Secker's, smudged features. Perplexed, his eyes raised. "Hell," he commented, "this was circulated four years back."

"Sure, but I've got a line on the jasper."

"Doubt if we want him now," protested the sheriff. "Witnesses are scattered, likely the records are lost. This case is as dead as last year's calendar."

"You lost interest in a fugitive killer?"

The sheriff smiled tiredly. "Hell, we average a homicide a week."

"I'm not pushing for prosecution, or even claiming the bounty money," explained Moreland. "All I crave is to get a line on

Secker's background — where he hailed from, how come he got involved in the knifing fracas, who he knifed."

Hall switched on his tolerant smile. "Young feller, I don't even recollect this killing, and doubt if anyone else does. You're flogging a dead horse." He glanced over Moreland's shoulder as two deputies approached, wrestling with a yelling, struggling prisoner, and thrust out a hand. "Wal, it was sure nice meeting you."

The interview was plainly at an end.

XV

Despondent, Moreland drifted along the plankwalk, heedless of his surroundings, carried along by the tide of men. He had been loco, he told himself, to build up expectations. As Hall had pointed out, a busy sheriff had neither the time nor inclination to exhume cases that had been dead for years. Likely the record in the Secker case had gone into the ashcan way back. He had played a hunch and it had misfired. All he could do now was forget the whole thing and board the next stage back to Lennox.

After a while he became aware that the press of men had thinned and he was passing darkened store fronts. The hell-raising seemed confined to an area centered by the saloons at the southerly end of the street. Sound of steady pounding reached his ears. Curiosity aroused, he checked in front of a square brick building. Light from the interior silhouetted the words TUCSON STAR inscribed across a dusty window pane. Peering, the deputy glimpsed a man wearing an ink-daubed apron standing beside a massive flatbed press. At a table nearby a younger man, felt hat askew, cigarette drooping from a corner of his mouth, was scribbling furiously. Type cases bulked in the background and a medley of books, papers, printing plates were heaped untidily on side shelves. Balled paper, cigarette butts and burnt matches littered the floor.

An idea sparked in Moreland's mind. He pushed open the door and approached the felt-hatted scribbler at the table. A sheet of paper, pasted on its side, carried the words *Al. Durham, Editor.*

"Say," inquired the deputy, "how long this sheet been published?"

"Nine years," the editor told him, without pausing in his writing. "Back issues four bits."

"You keep a copy of every issue?" persisted the deputy.

"Sure!" The editor looked up. His lips

twisted humorously. "Preserved for posterity!"

"Could I look over issues around" — Moreland consulted the dodger — "June, 1868?"

"We'd be honored," the other assured him, straightfaced. He scraped back his chair and stepped over to a crowded shelf. He returned lugging a big bound volume with both hands. With a thump, he dropped it on the table. "Take my seat," he invited; "I've got to beat it down to the Gray Mule — some floozy brained a gambler with a whiskey bottle." With that, he hit for the street.

Moreland dropped onto the chair, opened up the bound volume of *The Tucson Star* for 1868 and commenced to thumb through it.

Finally, he found the item he sought, squeezed into the tail end of a column beneath a long account of a Hibernian picnic. It read:

SALOON STABBING

Jonas Secker, itinerant, is sought by the sheriff on a charge of homicide. Secker is accused of stabbing one John Hawker in the Buckhorn Saloon. Deputy Broadbill testified that Hawker was dead when he arrived but witnesses named Secker as his assailant. Both men were apparently engaged in a dispute when Secker suddenly drew a knife, stabbed Hawker and fled.

It wasn't much, but it gave Moreland the lead he wanted. Now he had to try to locate Deputy Broadbill.

When he reentered the sheriff's office and Hall focused him, the expression of weary tolerance stamped on the lawman's features became even more marked. It was apparent he'd hoped that he'd seen the last of the inquisitive deputy from Culver County.

"Just one more question, Sheriff," said Moreland hastily, "and I'll make myself scarce. Is Deputy Broadbill around?"

"Sure!" said Hall. "Bill's on night watch."

"He handled the Secker stabbing. Mind if I brace him?"

"Nope!" The sheriff's voice held obvious relief. He glanced at a clock high on the wall. "Bill's due in ten minutes. Rest your legs!"

Broadbill proved to be a heavy-set man, with lumpy jaws, a thick moustache and a frowning stare. He looked tough and belligerent, but when Moreland made his mission known, he proved cooperative, as far as he was able.

"The Hawker case," he rumbled. "Sure I remember it. Secker cut him up and ducked out; never did see hide nor hair of the jasper again."

"You know where Secker hailed from?"

"Texas, according to talk."

"He tied in with the Garrote Gang?"

Broadbill looked puzzled. "Never did hear of that bunch," he confessed. Then he brightened. "Now you bring it up, seems a barkeep did say he heard Hawker accuse Secker of garroting. Never had come up against that word before and it kinda stuck in my mind."

"That all?" Moreland was all attention now.

"Yep, except that Hawker was a Pinkerton dick. We found a badge in his pants pocket. The sheriff sent a report East, but nothing ever come of it."

"I'm sure thanking you!" Moreland's voice was tight with excitement. The pattern was plain now — a Pinkerton operative had braced Secker, alias Bigfoot, in the saloon, likely accused him of being a fugitive member of the Garrote Gang. Bigfoot had panicked, stabbed the other to death and fled.

In high spirits, the deputy returned to his hotel. He had garnered enough evidence now to tie in Bigfoot with Heckel's murder. First he'd killed in Tucson to escape capture, then again in Mustang. Likely he recognized Heckel as the turncoat member of the gang and garroted him in a derisive gesture of vengeance. It all fitted as neatly as a .45 shell into the cylinder of a Colt.

When he rode into Mustang it seemed that he had been absent for weeks, although actually just five days had elapsed since he'd set out for Tucson. It was late afternoon and long shadows fingered across the square. Sheriff Robinson hunched in front of the law shack, chair tilted back against it, as always. The sheriff, thought Moreland, was as much a fixture as a cigar store Indian, and just about as inactive. Well, with the information he'd brought back, Robinson would have no excuse for refusing to get busy.

He stabled the black, stripped off its rigging, strolled around front and hunkered nearby Robinson.

"How was Tucson?" inquired the sheriff, with no other greeting.

"Daytime it just sizzles," returned the deputy, "nights it goes hogwild." Unable to bottle his exhilaration any longer, he burst out, "I got the goods on Bigfoot. That bustard was a member of the Garrote Gang."

"You don't say!" Robinson's tone held flat disinterest.

"Four years back he knifed a Pinkerton man who tried to arrest him in Tucson. He took it on the lam, strayed up here. Heckel, alias Buckskin O'Brien, rides in. Bigfoot reads his brand, strangles him for a double-crosser."

"Maybe," suggested the sheriff mildly, "you should spread your hand. You got proof of all this?"

"Plenty!" asserted Moreland. He told of the newspaper item and his talk with Deputy Broadbill.

When he was through, Robinson tapped out his pipe, straightened his chair and came to his feet. "Seems Bigfoot got some explaining to do," he declared.

"I'll go round up the maverick," offered Moreland eagerly, and jumped up.

"You stick right here!" directed the sheriff, and there was a quality in his tone that indicated he would brook no argument.

Reluctantly, the deputy stood watching Robinson's chunky figure fade as he stumped off into the gathering gloom, cutting across the square in the direction of the livery.

He'd done all the work, reflected Moreland morosely, and now Robinson had taken the case out of his hands. The sheriff plainly didn't intend to allow a raw deputy to grab the prestige for cracking the Heckel case.

In no good humor, Moreland dropped onto the sheriff's vacated chair and made a cigarette. At least, he consoled himself, he'd cleared his own name. Likely, too, Robinson would bring Bigfoot back to the law shack and they'd both interrogate him.

The shadows lengthened, gradually faded as night crept on. Eyeing the vague bulk of the livery as it slowly dissolved from view, Moreland bottled his impatience, expecting at any moment to see Bigfoot shamble through the gloom in custody of the sheriff.

Oncoming night blotted out the livery, light began blooming in windows of scattered shacks, but there was no sign of either.

Itchy now, Moreland began to pace to and fro, wondering what in creation could be holding up Robinson. The thought suddenly struck him that Bigfoot might have used his knife again and maybe the sheriff lay dying in the livery while his assailant made another getaway. Unable to restrain himself longer, he began loping across the square with ever-quickening stride.

He checked as a chunky form emerged from the livery, moved toward him. "Jim!" he exclaimed with heartfelt relief. "I sure figured you were cold meat, that Bigfoot had used a knife on you. Where is the lobo?"

"Danged ef I know," grunted Robinson. "I combed out that livery. He sure ain't around."

"Guess he lamped me when I rode in." Moreland's voice was flat with chagrin. "Likely figured I'd got a line on him in Tucson."

"Seems that way," agreed Robinson, an edge to his tone. It came to the deputy that the sheriff was more annoyed with him — Moreland — for prodding him into action than with his own failure to locate Bigfoot.

The sheriff's voice broke into his train of thought. "Guess I'll head for home. Phyllis gets awful prickly ef I'm late for supper. You keep cases on the livery. Bigfoot may duck back. From the looks of things he lit out in a hurry, left his blankets. Likely he'll need chuck, too."

"Sure will!" agreed Moreland eagerly. "I'll poke around, too. Maybe I'll get a line on the sidewinder."

If Bigfoot ducked back, he reflected, the liveryman would make it late, when he figured everyone in town was asleep. So he ate a leisurely supper, killed a little time in the saloon, then headed for the livery to commence his vigil.

Stars were bright overhead and a yellow glow illuminated the front of the saloon. Here and there lighted windows patched the night like peering eyes. The distant half-human shriek of a prowling mountain lion drifted down from the ridges and, for no good reason, sent a shiver down his spine. An eerie feeling gripped him that death was abroad that night.

Mentally cursing his qualms, he moved away from the row of darkened store buildings and headed across the square, the outline of the livery bulking faint ahead.

A hundred paces from the big barn he stopped, uncertain just where to take up position. Bigfoot could slip in the rear, he considered, but if he covered that the front would be wide open. He moved closer, until the small panes of glass in the barn sash that gave light to the liveryman's living quarters were not a dozen paces distant. Then he sank down and settled himself to wait.

Time dragged. Small fragments of sound drifted across the bare expanse of the square — the gritty rasp of the saloon batwings, the plaintive chirping of a circling night bird, the pawing of a pony. But nothing moved in the starlit night. Unthinking, the watcher began to build a cigarette, remembered it would be a clear giveaway and dropped paper and tobacco. Drowsiness began to smother his senses like an insidious drug. He'd pounded leather most of the day, riding up from Lennox, and had been able to grab only a few short snatches of sleep on the jouncing stage the previous night. It now seemed that the one thing he craved above everything was a little shuteye. Again and again he jerked up his nodding head, snapped awake and moved stiff limbs.

Abruptly, his languor vanished. Behind the barn sash window of the cubbyhole he glimpsed a flash of light, gleaming pale on the panes. Tensed, he watched. Again light winked behind the window, vanished. Someone was moving around that room, he decided, packing a shielded lamp. Likely it was Bigfoot, who had stolen back to gather up his belongings. The sheriff's hunch had paid off.

Quickly he came to his feet, moving cautiously toward the gaping rectangle of darkness that was the entrance to the barn. Crouched, he slid along the clapboards to the doorway of the cubbyhole. Groping, he found the doorknob, threw the door back and jumped inside — was conscious of someone behind him. Before he could turn, a cord enveloped his neck, tightened, ruthlessly cutting into his throat. In a flash, realization came that he was marked for the same death as Heckel. Desperately he clawed at the taut thong, the heavy breathing of his attacker loud in his ears. Kicking, wrenching, swaying, he fought to break free. But his assailant clung like a leech and the strangling thong bit deeper. Congested, the blood thundered against his eardrums; his brain whirled in a vortex of darkness; his mouth gaped as his starved lungs fought for air. Consciousness slid away — he dropped down, down, down into a black abyss.

XVI

Lungs heaving, Moreland fought for breath. It seemed that he was immersed in the depths of a yellow ocean, starved of air, held down by remorseless pressure on his back. Then he grasped that he was stretched out on a grimy dirt floor, face downward, and two strong hands were rhythmically compressing and releasing his ribs. Gasping spasmodically, he rolled over — to focus the bearded features of Paul the Preacher, plain in the yellow light of a smoky stable lamp. He lay wheezing, blinking at the preacher, striving to comprehend the strange situation. Recollection began to flow back — the attack, the strangling thong cutting into his windpipe, the descent into darkness.

Paul came to his feet, reached down, grabbed both his arms and hoisted Moreland up, steered him to the truckle bed. Thankfully, he dropped down upon it, fingering his throat. It felt as though it were banded by a red-hot wire. Painfully he croaked, "What in creation's going on?"

"The good Lord hath seen fit to make me the instrument of His mercy, brother, and preserve your miserable life." The preacher's voice boomed like a bass drum. "I was entering the barn to rest my weary bones upon the straw pile when sound of a struggle drew me to this room. In the darkness, a man scuttled past me, elusive as a rat. I lit the lamp and you were lying on the floor, near death, till I pumped air into your lungs."

"Bigfoot!" muttered Moreland. "The bustard tolled me inside and lay for me. I'm sure thanking you, Preacher. The rattlesnake throttled Heckel, and 'most got me."

"Thank your Creator!" boomed Paul. "Be

grateful that in His divine wisdom He hath seen fit to extend the span of your unworthy existence."

"Wal, I'm thanking you both," Moreland assured him fervently and became aware that he was producing no more than a hoarse whisper from his damaged throat. He came uncertainly to his feet. "Guess I'll get back to my room."

"You are easy prey, brother, if the miscreant is lurking outside," cautioned Paul. "Verily you walk in the shadow of death. The good Lord would have me side you to your resting place."

"You'll hear no objections from me," the deputy assured him, with a drawn smile. He felt so doggoned weak, he reflected, that he couldn't lick his upper lip.

The preacher blew out the lamp and together they moved out upon the creaky planks of the runway.

When they paced across the square, the night was still and the settlement darkened, except for a mellow glow behind the windows of the saloon. Outside the hotel, Moreland paused. "This is it," he said. "I'm sure plenty in your debt, Preacher."

"The devil is abroad tonight, brother, and maybe lurking in your room. Lead, I will follow."

"Heck," protested the deputy, "I gamble Bigfoot's running so fast his axles are heating."

But the preacher waved him on and the bearded man had a forceful way with him.

They crossed the deserted lobby, and the preacher dogged Moreland down the passageway and into his room. The deputy hooked his hat on a peg and his visitor dropped the big black Bible he packed in the crook of an arm upon the bed and plunked down beside it. He fished in the tails of his shabby frock coat, brought out the makin's and began adroitly fashioning a cigarette with long, flexible fingers. "Brother," he said, "I am curious." Moreland noted that his voice had lost its evangelistic boom. He spoke in crisp, matter-of-fact tones. "I am told that this county is a hideaway for lawless men, yet they observe the law. But tonight there was close to a killing and you speak of another man throttled. What excites this violence?"

"I been stirring up the Garrote Gang," returned the deputy grimly. He dropped into the only chair and told the whole story.

"Tonight," he concluded, "I kept cases on the livery, figuring he might sneak back." He grinned ruefully and touched his red-wealed neck. "The coyote sure did!"

The preacher listened intently, his dark, piercing eyes dwelling on the deputy. When Moreland was through, he commented, "Man is born to trouble. You tread a dangerous trail, brother. I know of these wolves. There are three at large. They strike swiftly and without mercy, as you well know. A wise man would —" His words cut off as a window pane shattered. Falling glass tinkled. Moreland heard the drone of a bullet and ducked — after it had embedded itself in the jamb of the door behind his head. The sharp spang of a Winchester resounded in his ears.

Paul had rolled off the bed. Moreland jumped for the lighted lamp on the bureau, doused it. Snatching out his gun, he ran toward the window. Paul was close behind him and he saw that a long-barreled Colt .45 was latched in the preacher's right fist.

Nothing moved outside as they stood peering through the broken window, fringed by a ragged framework of jagged glass.

"A persistent hornet, this son of Beliel," said Paul. "As I was about to say, brother, it would be wise to leave. He will try again."

"I'm sticking!" declared Moreland, his husky voice a trifle shaky. That persistent slug from the night had missed his head by an inch or so, and set his already jangled nerves quivering.

"Fools die for want of wisdom," returned Paul indifferently. He brushed back his frock coat and dropped the Colt into leather. His strong lips curved into a bleak smile. "Adios! May your dreams be pleasant." With long strides, he moved to the doorway and out of the room.

Taking no chances, Moreland yanked off his boots by faint light that filtered through the broken window, jammed the back of the straightback chair beneath the doorknob, slipped his six-gun beneath the pillow and stretched out on the bed. But sleep was denied him. The weal around his bruised throat burned like slow fire and a turmoil of thought coursed through his brain.

There was no doubt in his mind that Bigfoot would try again, as the preacher had warned — the liveryman had already made two stabs at bedding him down that night. Trouble was, there could be two more former members of the Garrote Gang around. They, too, were liable to strike. If he could only get hold of those old wanted dodgers and establish their identity he would have a chance to defend himself. Now he felt as helpless as a rabbit in a wolf's jaw.

This preacher was a queer cuss, too.

Packed a six-gun and made a cigarette as slick as any cowpoke. And how come he knew there were three members of the Garrote Gang still around?

Moreland's thoughts returned to the would-be assassin. It was plain that Bigfoot would get him if he didn't tag Bigfoot first. The odds favored the liveryman. Daytime he could duck into hiding, far enough from town to avoid possible capture; nights he could skulk around, waiting another chance to kill.

A hunch as to where his hideaway might be struck the restless deputy — Larner's cabin, beyond Cow Creek. The sheriff had given the horse thief marching orders, so the place would probably be abandoned. It was isolated and what neighbors there were were old lags, tending strictly to their own business. Bigfoot and Larner had been close, so the liveryman would probably know of it. A checkup could pay dividends.

Which was why Moreland rode out of Mustang at sunup.

It was noon when he reached Cow Creek. As before, he turned down stream, following the faint trail that meandered beside its gurgling course. Fresh hoof marks in boggy spots told that another rider had recently

146

passed that way. Spirits rising, the deputy pushed ahead. He'd stake his saddle that rider was Bigfoot.

At the fork of the creek he angled off along the now-familiar trail. As before, he tied his pony at a spot where it was well screened by chaparral. Easing through the brush, he worked toward the cabin. When he glimpsed it an exclamation of surprise left his lips. Slacked on the bench set across its front were two men, Bigfoot and Larner.

Nonplussed, he stood in the cover of the chaparral eyeing the pair. It had never entered his mind that the horse thief would ignore the sheriff's order to hightail. Just how should he handle this? he cogitated. He could return to the black, bring back his rifle and, with luck, pick off one or the other. At that, it was long range for a Winchester. And the idea didn't appeal: it would be mighty close to bushwhacking. What was more, he wanted Bigfoot alive. The liveryman represented his only chance of proving his innocence in the Heckel murder case.

He could head back to Mustang and enlist the sheriff's aid, but it was a long ride and Bigfoot might have vanished when they returned. Seemed all he could do was stick around and keep cases on the pair, hoping one or the other would ride out. With no enthusiasm, he settled himself to wait.

Shadows lengthened as the sun dropped westward. Cramped from his long watch, the deputy fretted behind his screen of brush and watched oncoming night begin to erase the cabin. Light bloomed in its windows.

During the dragging afternoon hours neither of the two men had given any indication of leaving. They seemed to be content to do nothing but kill time, wandering aimlessly in and out of the cabin, smoking, drifting around.

Wearying of waiting, Moreland began ghosting closer. Gun in hand, he eased up to the cabin, snatched a glance through a window. The two men hunched on chairs, facing each other across a small plank table on which a coal-oil lamp was set, cigarettes stuck between their lips as they slapped greasy cards. Seemed, he reflected, they had settled down for the night.

An urge for action suddenly possessed him, born of the frustration that had been building during those hours of watching and waiting. Thumbing back the hammer of his .45, he edged toward the half open door. Gun leveled, he kicked it back, jumped inside. "Reach!" he barked.

Two heads swiveled. No expression showed on Larner's eroded features, but Moreland saw his thin lips compress beneath the drooping moustache. Bigfoot's jaw dropped. Neither made a move.

"Hoist 'em!" gritted Moreland, standing tensed by the doorway.

Bigfoot's hands shot shoulder-high. Larner's left arm swung, swept the lamp off the table. The light blinked out as it crashed to the floor. Even while the broken glass clattered, a gun blared, its report thunderous in the small cabin, the muzzle flash briefly illuminating the room. Moreland caught a glimpse of one form flattened beyond the table, a second crouched, triggering. Even before the flash died, the six-gun boomed again. Moreland heard the flat slap of a slug against the wall behind him, dropped onto one knee and began spewing lead blindly in the direction of the crouched form. The cabin reverberated with the roar of gunfire, a deafening drumfire that beat against the deputy's ears. A fog of acrid powdersmoke, pierced by spearing flame, fouled the air. A shriek of mortal agony lanced into Moreland's eardrums and, at the same moment, a metallic click told him that his gun was empty. Then he became aware that the shooting had stopped. Eyes smarting from the powder fumes, he stared into darkness. He heard labored coughing, then Bigfoot's husky accents. "I quit!"

Moreland thought fast. He held an empty gun. When he answered both men would likely throw lead in the direction of his voice. Then he remembered the shriek.

He flattened against the earth floor. "Walk out," he yelled, "with your hands up." With that, he rolled, quickly.

A vague form materialized out of drifting powdersmoke, arms raised, shambled through the doorway. Moreland jumped up, leaped after it, braced for the impact of a bullet in the back. But no gunshot ripped the silence.

Reaching, he lifted Bigfoot's gun out of the holster, stuck it beneath his own waistband. Then he grabbed the liveryman's shoulder and spun him around. "Larner hit?" he demanded.

"Larner's dead!" Indignation shrilled Bigfoot's voice. "You kill crazy?"

"Yank the jasper out," directed Moreland, still leery of a trick.

As Bigfoot stood irresolute, he jammed the muzzle of his empty gun into the other's belly. "Maybe you prefer a slug," he snapped.

Reluctantly, the liveryman shuffled back

into the smoke-filled shack. Moreland grabbed the opportunity to plug out his empties and reload.

Bigfoot emerged, coughing, dragging Larner's limp form by the feet. One glance told Moreland that this was no fake. The horse thief's features were a bloody smear. It seemed a slug had carried away his entire lower jaw. Bigfoot dropped the legs. As he turned, hacking, the deputy fished a pair of handcuffs from a hip pocket. Before the liveryman realized his intent, he snapped them on the man's scrawny wrists.

"What's the charge?" demanded Bigfoot, with surly anger.

"Murder!" bit back Moreland. "You forgot Mike Heckel?"

"Now I know you're loco," grunted the prisoner.

"If you're not guilty how come you beat it?"

Bigfoot stood scowling, saying nothing.

"And how come you 'most throttled me in the barn last night?"

"I was right here last night!"

"Says you!"

"I got an ali—" Bigfoot checked, gazing gloomily at Larner's body, sprawled in the starlight. "There's my alibi — dead as Santa Anna."

XVII

In high good humor, Moreland stepped into the eating house, slapped his hat on a peg and dropped onto a stool, whistling.

"You got a reprieve or something?" inquired the perky waitress. "You're acting like the cat who just swallowed the canary."

"I got Heckel's killer in the lockup," he told her airily.

"You don't say! Who did strangle that poor man?" she asked curiously.

"You'd never guess," he grinned. "Gimme a stack o' flapjacks and 'lasses."

She tossed her head and retired to the kitchen. When she set his breakfast before him, she pleaded, "Give! Who killed Heckel?"

"Bigfoot!" he threw back. "I figure he's a member of the Garrote Gang."

"Figure!" the girl exclaimed. "You should know!"

The deputy sighed. If he swore he was innocent of the Cottonwood killing on a stack of Bibles, he thought, Milly Hogan wouldn't believe him, and somehow it would mean a heap to clear himself in her eyes.

"Yep, this is why I know!" he barked, and opened his shirt at the neck. Tilting back his head, he exposed the dull red ring around his throat. "Bigfoot!" he said shortly. "The bustard almost beefed me."

"Why?" The girl stood eyeing the red weal with shocked attention.

"Because I had him dead to rights," he told her grimly. "Got the lowdown in Tucson. Heckel was a member of the gang — once. The law corralled him. He drew a short term for ratting on his pards. When he came out of stir he turned bounty hunter."

"And rode into Mustang hunting blood money?"

"Or a showdown; I ain't sure which. My guess is that Bigfoot read his brand and beefed him for a double-crosser. What's more, I'm hoping the lobo'll crack and clear me of the Cottonwood charge."

"You know, Sam, I'm beginning to think that maybe you were unjustly convicted," she murmured, gray eyes thoughtful.

"If you had the brains of a bumblebee you'd never have nursed any doubts," he returned indulgently.

"I said maybe!" she snapped, and picked up his empty mug. Warily he eyed her until she'd refilled it at the urn and banged it down in front of him.

As he ate, the girl stood watching him. Suddenly, she inquired, "Weren't there four members of the Garrote Gang — counting you out?"

"That's what folks claim."

"So there are still two on the loose. Aren't you in danger?"

He shrugged carelessly. "I doubt if they're around."

Breakfast under his belt, the deputy headed for the barn that served as lockup. Midnight had long passed when he'd returned to Mustang with his prisoner and he'd decided there was no point in dragging the sheriff out of bed. So he'd jugged Bigfoot and gone to grab a little shut-eye.

When he steered the sullen prisoner across the square now, the sheriff's chunky form lumped on his tilted chair outside the office. Impassively, Robinson listened to his deputy's account of the throttling attempt in the livery barn, the bushwhack shot through the hotel window, the fracas in Larner's cabin.

"So I finally rounded this rattlesnake up," concluded Moreland triumphantly. "Guess we got an open-and-shut case."

"You got anything to say?" inquired the sheriff of Bigfoot.

The prisoner merely spat disgust.

"Lock him up!" directed Robinson.

Moreland conducted his prisoner back

across the square to the barn behind the general store, which was all Mustang had to offer in the way of a jail. Reaching the barn, he shifted Bigfoot's handcuffs from his wrists to his ankles, closed the door and dropped the bar that secured it into place. Legging back to the law shack, he remembered the waitress' remark about two Garrote Gang members still being on the loose.

"Could be Bigfoot's got two pards skulking around," he pointed out, when he reached the office. "A kid could bust into that barn. The coyote should be guarded."

"Quit fretting!" advised Robinson shortly. "He's safe till sundown; then I'll keep cases on the lobo."

Moreland brightened. "I'll relieve you at midnight," he offered.

"Suits me!" The sheriff's voice held flat indifference.

Robinson was sure as sullen as a sore-headed dog, reflected Moreland. The sheriff said nothing more, just sat there, smoking, and the deputy was in no mood for further talk.

Moreland felt his head nodding. Now the excitement was over, reaction seemed to have set in. He felt limp as a wet sack, drained of energy. It wasn't surprising, he considered; he sure was short on sleep. He hadn't grabbed more than eight hours' shut-eye in the past two nights.

He could see that news of the liveryman's arrest was percolating around. Knots of men were gathered outside the store and the saloon. Although they were too far distant for their talk to reach his ears, he could guess from their gestures that they were arguing. Likely about the prisoner's guilt, he reflected, and could be Bigfoot's two pards were among them. Impulsively, he remarked to Robinson, "If we could get hold of them Garrote Gang dodgers it would sure ease things up around here."

The sheriff merely grunted.

The old buffalo acted like he didn't give a damn, mused Moreland. If someone took a shot at him when he was on guard after nightfall maybe he'd change his ideas.

The preacher's unkempt form came into view. Astride a shaggy mule, he angled across the square in their direction. Something seemed different about the bearded evangelist and Moreland turned to ask the sheriff about it. Robinson seemed engrossed in the approaching rider, his gaze fixed, speculation in his blunt gray eyes.

The preacher pulled close. Checking the mule, he sat the saddle, stroking his long beard. "Brethren," he intoned, "I am sunk in a bog of desolation. I have mislaid my staff, my right arm, my comfort and guide."

"That big Bible," guessed Moreland.

"Yes, indeed," admitted the preacher despondently. "You will remember, brother, that we were distracted by unseemly events in the livery some two nights back, and again in your hotel room. Unthinking, I must have set it down."

"Too bad!" sympathized the deputy. "You hunted?"

"Everywhere," sighed Paul. "The good woman at the hotel assures me that if she saw a Bible in your room, brother, she would never forget it. I have combed the livery barn, in vain. Alas, that I should be cursed with such forgetfulness."

"It'll come to light," said Moreland.

"Only that hope sustains me," responded the preacher dolefully. Wheeling away, he abruptly checked the mule. "It has come to me that my wretched memory failed again," he confessed, glumly eyeing the deputy. "When I passed through Lennox, heading for this seething caldron of sin, the good sheriff sent a message. It seems you were searching for dodgers describing three sinful men."

"The Garrote Gang," supplied Moreland.

"He telegraphed to Myberg, Texas. It

seems that the dodgers are available and have been dispatched by mail."

"Say!" exclaimed the deputy eagerly. "That's the best news I've had in a coon's age. When you figure Lanker will get his hands on them?"

"Very soon, I would say, brother," returned Paul. He raised his reins and heeled the mule.

"You hear that, Jim?" Moreland turned to the sheriff as the evangelist drifted away. "Seems we're about to get a line on the lobos."

Robinson nodded absently, engrossed in his own thoughts.

Moreland yawned, again fighting lassitude. If he didn't get some sleep, he thought, he'd never keep awake when he took over guard duty at midnight. Robinson sure didn't give any indication that he craved company. It might be a smart idea to grab a little shut-eye.

"What shenanigans you been up to?" Mrs. Larcombe wanted to know, when he entered the hotel lobby. "There's a broken pane in your window, and that crazy preacher has been around claiming he left a Bible in your room. Then there's talk you got Bigfoot penned up."

"When I got time I'll wise you up." He grinned. "There's been happenings, big happenings in Mustang."

"I can't even keep up with happenings in this hotel," she grumbled. "Don't blame me if the room's drafty, and don't squawk at your next bill. Window glass comes high."

But Moreland's thoughts were not on window glass, only sleep.

Gratefully, he closed the door of his room, scaled his hat into a corner, yanked off his boots and stretched out on the bed. In dreamy contentment, he lay musing on the crowded events of the past few days. At last he was nearing the goal that had brought him to Mustang. . . . In minutes he was sleeping, so soundly that nothing less than a thunderclap would have awakened him.

He woke up to stare into pitch darkness. Still drugged by sleep, he stumbled across to the bureau, found a block of stinkers and struck a match. The hands of his watch registered 11:21. He'd sure had a slug of sleep! Grateful that he'd awakened in plenty of time to relieve the sheriff at midnight, he lit the lamp, dropped down on the bed again and fumbled for the boots he'd dropped beside it. Groping blindly, he touched something hard, fingered it — and hauled Paul's big Bible from beneath the bed. Must

159

have been kicked there in the darkness when the bushwhack bullet had plunked through the window, he reflected. Paul had rolled off the bed and the Bible had likely rolled with him. Well, the find would make the preacher happy. Idly, he opened the Bible, began flipping through its pages. There seemed to be a bulge inside the black cover. He investigated, and eyed an envelope, stuck to the cover. From it protruded the ends of several yellow sheets. Curiously, he slid them out — and gasped with a shock of surprise. In his hand were three wanted dodgers, and the topmost bore a reproduction of Sheriff Robinson's rugged features. The dodger named him "Dutch," boss of the Garrote Gang, and the reward was five thousand dollars — dead or alive. Wide awake now, the bewildered Moreland examined the two remaining dodgers. One carried Bigfoot's wizened features, the other those of Ted Larner, the horse thief.

XVIII

Still battling bewilderment, Moreland sat eyeing the dodgers. It was plain enough now why the sheriff was reluctant to cooperate and why he had allowed Bigfoot to slip through his fingers. But how come the preacher was packing the dodgers? Then he remembered that Robinson was supposedly guarding the prisoner. He jammed the dodgers in a pocket, pulled on his boots, grabbed his gunbelt in furious haste and tornadoed out of the room.

At a run, he drummed over the deserted plankwalk, ducked into the alley beside the general store — a narrow canyon of darkness — and raced down it. The barn bulked vaguely on a debris-littered lot. He jerked out his gun, picked his way through discarded boxes and barrels, alert for trouble. But no one seemed to be around. The barn door gaped open. Careless of a trap, he charged inside. Rats skittered, that was all. The prisoner had vanished.

Uncertain of his next move, Moreland stepped outside, and whirled at sound of a footstep. Paul's gaunt form loomed in the faint light.

"Brother," intoned the preacher, "the bird has flown."

"What's it to you?" snapped the deputy.

"I had hoped to save his immortal soul," returned the preacher blandly.

"Quit hurrahin' me!" bit back the deputy. He yanked out the three dodgers. "The Garrote Gang! Stuck in the back of your Bible. How come?"

The preacher smiled. "Just three black sheep, brother," he averred. "I had hopes of returning them to the fold."

"You're lying!" accused Moreland. "I got you pegged as a bounty hunter and that preaching rig a fake. You were hellbent to collect fifteen thousand in bounty money — five thousand apiece."

"Could be," returned Paul, unabashed. His tone changed, became crisp, incisive. "You want 'em, to clear your record. I want 'em, to claim the blood money. If we don't work in double harness, neither will collect." There was no trace of the florid Biblical language now.

"So?" questioned Moreland.

"The lobos have beat it. We go after 'em."

That was easier said than done, reflected the deputy. Who knew in what direction the fugitives had ridden? They'd have to guess, and likely guess wrong. "You got any ideas?" he inquired.

"Figure it from Dutch's angle," returned Paul. "That hombre's as slick as calf slobbers. He'll know that you'll spread the alarm, which means every trail and waterhole between here and the border will be watched. So he'll just naturally head elsewhere. East, at a guess."

"Yeah!" mocked Moreland. "Over them

mountains?" He jerked his head in the direction of the Chiricahuas.

"You forgot Horseshoe Pass?"

"Never heard of it."

"I gamble Dutch has," threw back Paul. "It's a high pass, too narrow for stages, a back door into New Mexico. Lies twenty-five — thirty miles northeast. In Dutch's boots, I'd hit for the Pass."

"Let's go!" snapped Moreland.

Shadows in the starlight, the two pulled out of Mustang, riding north, Moreland content to follow the pseudo-preacher's lead.

At dawn they halted on the bank of a bouldery creek to rest and water the animals. Welcoming the respite themselves, the two men hunkered, smoking and trading talk.

In the half-light, tails of his frock coat dragging, head hunched between his shoulders, nose curving out like a beak, Paul reminded the deputy of nothing so much as a big, brooding vulture. Some intuition warned him that Paul was cooking up something on his own hook. What it could be he had no idea; he just couldn't bring himself to wholly trust the hombre.

The bearded man's gaze lit on him. "So you figure," he said, "that Bigfoot beefed

163

this Heckel hombre, and 'most throttled you?" He had dropped his pious intonation as carelessly as a man might drop a cloak when it had served his purpose.

Moreland nodded.

"You're dead wrong," declared Paul. "When the gang was operating Dutch handled the garroting, and I gamble he still handles it. Bigfoot just wouldn't have the guts. You recollect Buckskin O'Brien was crippled by a slug in Myberg and corralled? The rest of the gang skeedaddled, left Buckskin cold. He got sore, spilled his guts and the law let him off easy — five years. The jasper had five years to chew on the fact that his pards crossed him and got away with his share of the loot. I'm gambling he left the pen in a sod-pawing, horn-tossing mood."

"Sounds reasonable," agreed the deputy.

"I'd say," continued Paul, "he nursed one notion — to even up with Dutch. Dutch always called the turn; when he cracked the whip his boys jumped, and I don't mean maybe. So Buckskin changes his name to Heckel and turns bounty hunter, which gives him a license to poke around."

"And Dutch read his brand just as soon as he hit Mustang," put in the deputy, remembering how quickly the sheriff had dabbed out of sight to "fix a latch" at his home when the stranger rode in. He recalled Heckel's words in the Wagon Wheel, too: "I figure on punching the breeze, just as soon as I've evened up with a certain yellow-gutted coyote."

"Why wouldn't he?" retorted Paul. "Buckskin rode like a cavalryman, walked with a limp and packed his gun on the left side."

"And he had a hunch Dutch was around," mused Moreland. "Dutch had to put out his light or he was through as sheriff, likely through for keeps. It was a cinch to keep cases on the saloon and throttle the poor bustard when he left. Then he locates my dodger in Heckel's saddlebags and does his damndest to pin the killing on me."

Paul smiled, showing strong white teeth. "That's just how I read it. Then you upset the applecart by riding down to Lennox and getting the straight on Heckel. That bothered Dutch, and when you tied Bigfoot in with the Garrote Gang he figures it's time to close your yap for keeps. It was Dutch tolled you into the livery. It so happened I was keeping cases on the lobo and queered the throttling deal."

Moreland eyed his companion, brow creased. "You had the gang spotted, how come you didn't bring in the law and jug 'em?"

Paul eyed him blandly. "For good reason. Maybe I'll make it plain — later." He straightened, stretched. "Guess we should amble along."

At sundown they made their last halt before tackling the Pass. Both animals were gaunted and Moreland was so bone-weary that with every jolt of his pony he felt he was falling apart. But, after a breather, Paul insisted upon pressing on. If their quarry crossed into New Mexico Territory, he pointed out, all chance of picking up their tracks would be lost — they'd vanish into a wide spread of wild country. He was banking that, feeling secure from pursuit, the pair would camp for the night in the Pass. They'd had a tough ride, too.

The mountains overshadowed them now, great masses of granite, bulging into craggy heights, spires and domes. Then, suddenly, they passed through the portals of the Pass and darkness enveloped them. On either side, eroding rock walls hemmed them in. High above their heads, the sky was a ragged ribbon of fading blue. The hooves of their plodding mounts stirred up a fog of fine talus dust. Like gray ghosts, they plugged through the deep defile that knifed through the mountains.

Paul, riding ahead, abruptly pulled rein. Moreland drifted up to his stirrup. Ahead, a faint red glow pricked through the gloom.

"We drew aces!" breathed the deputy.

"Now we got to play the hand," said Paul. He stepped down, slid his Winchester out of the boot, blew the dust off its breach.

"What's the play?" inquired Moreland.

Paul raised his broad shoulders. "Mosey in. If we've hit the jackpot, blast 'em."

"You mean beef the jaspers?"

"Dead or alive, they're still worth five thousand apiece," said Paul carelessly. He might, thought Moreland, have been discussing a couple of steers.

"No killing!" objected the deputy.

The bearded man eyed him, plainly puzzled. "Why in creation would we take 'em alive?" he inquired. "They'll pack easier dead."

"Because I need their testimony," explained the deputy. "We close their mouths for keeps and I spend the rest of my life on the dodge, or rotting in Huntsville."

Paul considered this, frowning. "Hunky-dory!" he agreed at length. "Now how you crave to handle it?"

"Injun close in and throw down on the lobos."

"Dutch is chain lightning with a six-gun."

"I go in — you cover Dutch."

Paul shrugged. "You're crazy as a bedbug, but have it the way you want."

They hobbled their mounts and shucked spurs. Paul packing his Winchester, the two began to leg through the darkness, talus dust, ankle-deep, muffling their footsteps like a thick carpet.

Their pace slowed as they drew closer to a tiny camp fire. By its flickering light, Moreland focused on the sheriff — it was still hard to think of him as Dutch — hunched by it, watching a sooted coffee pot, set to boil. Across from him, Bigfoot's wizened features were plain. Close by, their ponies made lumpy shadows. Paul touched Moreland's arm and melted into the gloom. Lifting his .45 out of leather, the deputy eased ahead.

XIX

Unobserved, Moreland approached to within a dozen paces of the fire. The sharp click, as he thumbed back the hammer of the Colt, brought both renegades' heads around as though jerked by a single string.

"Hands up!" he snapped, moving into the circle of light.

Both slowly came to their feet.

Bigfoot's arms wavered upward but the sheriff, fast as a striking rattlesnake, dabbed for his .45. As his right arm blurred down, the report of a gunshot echoed and reechoed against the confining walls. Robinson staggered, his arms dropped limp and the gun spilled from his fingers. Like a punctured waterbag, he collapsed, crashed down. His blocky frame quivered once, then was still.

Bigfoot, straining his arms high, was yelling frantically, "Don't shoot!"

Moreland stepped up to the liveryman, slipped the buckle of his gunbelt and swung it clear. Then he fished out a pair of handcuffs and snapped them on Bigfoot's wrists. A stream of bitter invective flowed from the renegade's lips.

"Button!" growled the deputy and slanted his gun on the wizened hardcase. "You're worth just as much dead as alive." Bigfoot's profanity promptly cut off. Tight-lipped, he glowered at his captor.

Paul emerged from the shadows. He carelessly kicked the sheriff's six-gun away from a slack hand and stirred the sprawled form with a boot toe. "Guess the hairpin's dancing a jig in Hell," he said offhand, set his

Winchester against a rock and became busy rummaging through the renegades' gear.

Moreland stood eyeing him, puzzled. "What you expect to find?" he inquired.

"This!" threw back Paul, an odd note of excitement in his tone. He held up a bulging buckskin pouch. As Moreland watched, he untied a thong that secured its neck, tilted it and spilled a cascade of scintillating stones into a palm.

He looked up, lips curling with amusement at the surprise registered on the deputy's features.

"Loot of the Garrote Gang," he explained, "converted to diamonds. Easy to pack, easy to hide."

"I'll be damned!" exclaimed Moreland. He held out a hand. "Guess I'll take 'em," he said, "and turn 'em over to the law."

"Sure," returned Paul agreeably. "We'll split the bounty; it'll likely run to twenty percent of their value." He funneled the stones back into the pouch, retied it and tossed it to the deputy. Moreland stowed it in a pants pocket.

"Wal," continued Paul, in high good humor, "you bring up the saddle stock and I'll brew the coffee. This doggoned dust sure dries a man out."

Moreland nodded, and plugged away into

the darkness.

When he rode the black back, with Paul's mule on the lead, the bearded man was sipping a tin cup of steaming coffee. He held another to the deputy. "Bigfoot had a swig," he said apologetically, "but I swilled the cup out good." Moreland glanced at the prisoner. Slumped against a saddle, Bigfoot seemed to have fallen asleep. He swallowed the hot liquid gratefully.

It was dawn when he awoke and the cold of the high pass bit into his very marrow. Raising to a sitting position, he stared stupidly around, his brain foggy and his head as heavy as a chunk of lead. Bigfoot still flopped against the saddle, wrists manacled, snoring. Dutch's form was stiffening beyond the dead ashes of the fire. But there was no sign of Paul or his mule.

Unsteadily, the deputy came to his feet, peering around in the gray light, striving to marshal his thoughts. His last recollection was swallowing the mug of coffee Paul had handed him. Then he became aware that the pouch of diamonds was no longer in his pants pocket.

Understanding came. That coffee had contained a knockout drop. Paul had not been hunting bounties, but a far greater prize — the loot of the Garrote Gang. He'd promised to make things plain later. He sure had! By now, he had crossed the Pass and was beyond pursuit. Moreland couldn't repress a sickly grin. Intuition had warned him to beware the bearded man. The preacher was sure the slickest hombre he had ever come up against.

Wasting no time, he wrestled Dutch's body up on his pony, roped it securely into place. Then he rigged the two remaining ponies and booted Bigfoot into wakefulness. Bleary-eyed and still dazed, the prisoner climbed clumsily into the saddle without protest and sat slumped while the deputy secured his manacled wrists to the horn. This was no time, considered the deputy, to take chances. Then, with both ponies on the lead, Moreland began to retrace his trail westward.

It was a long, wearisome ride down to Lennox, but he pushed doggedly ahead, determined to get his prisoner into jail by nightfall and tell his story to Sheriff Lanker.

Darkness veiled the cow town when the little cavalcade jogged in. Moreland tied up outside the courthouse, steered Bigfoot up the brick steps and down the corridor.

The sheriff's office was empty except for Lanker, slacked at his desk, talking with a smooth-faced man garbed in a wrinkled store suit. Both looked up when Moreland entered, propelling the wizen-faced renegade before him.

Deadpan, Lanker eyed the dust-powdered deputy and his scowling prisoner. "Hunting a jail?" he inquired gravely.

"You said it!" threw back Moreland and dropped gratefully onto a chair. "You acquainted with this hombre?"

Lanker inspected the prisoner again. "Nope," he decided, "and I can't say I missed much."

"That's Carl Hager, late of the Garrote Gang, alias Jonas Secker, wanted for a knifing in Tucson, alias Bigfoot, Mustang liveryman. I got the corpse of Dutch, late boss of the Garrote Gang, alias Sheriff Robinson, lashed to his pony outside."

"I'll be double-damned!" exclaimed Lanker. "I wired Myberg for them dodgers."

"That's what Paul the Preacher told me."

"Paul the Preacher!" exclaimed the smooth-faced man. He dipped into an inside pocket, brought out a wanted dodger, handed it to the deputy. "I'm Fred Yates, Wells Fargo investigator," he volunteered. "This the preacher?"

Moreland eyed the sheet, gazed into the features of Paul, a younger-looking Paul, hair clipped short, clean-shaven. But there was no mistaking the strong jaw, broad brow, deep-set, piercing eyes. The deputy read:

$1,000 REWARD

will be paid for information leading to the apprehension of Mark Leighton, height 6'2"; weight 210; black hair; dark eyes. Wanted for homicide and bank robbery. Well educated, trained for the ministry. This man is dangerous. Send information to Wells Fargo & Co., 114 Montgomery Street, San Francisco, California, or any Wells Fargo agency.

"That's the hombre," said Moreland, "but he's grown a beard and wears his hair long."

"Where'll I find him?" inquired Yates eagerly.

"Somewhere in New Mexico Territory," said the deputy. He smiled. "It's quite a story."

"Spill it!" invited Lanker, and fished out papers and tobacco.

Moreland told of the events that had transpired in Mustang and his pursuit of Dutch and Bigfoot in the company of the preacher. "We caught up with 'em in Horseshoe Pass," he concluded. "Dutch drew and the preacher downed him. Then Paul dug a pouch of diamonds out of Dutch's saddle-bags."

"Loot!" put in Lanker.

The deputy nodded. "Wal, I claimed the stones to turn over to the law and Paul handed the pouch over without a squawk. Later, Paul feeds me a knockout drop and I wake up this a.m. with a sore head and no pouch. Paul had beat it."

"Too bad!" murmured Lanker. "Wal, you got ten thousand dollars in bounty money coming. That ain't chicken feed."

"I outslickered the hombre." Moreland couldn't repress a grin. "When I brought in the saddle stock I grabbed the chance to fill that pouch with pebbles." He reached down, lifted a knotted bandana from a boot top. Opening it up, he displayed a sparkling array of diamonds.

"Jesus!" gasped Lanker.

XX

When Moreland rode into Mustang, he headed straight for the eating house. Everything seemed normal, except that every townsman he passed had a question in his eyes.

"Hello, stranger!" greeted the waitress, when he slid onto a stool.

"Miss me?" he inquired.

"Maybe!" she replied with a toss of her head. "Where have you been? The whole town's talking. First you disappear with the sheriff, taking Bigfoot. Then the Empress suddenly decides to leave town, too. What does it all mean?"

"Draw me a mug of dip," said Moreland, "and I'll tell you a story that will knock your hat off."

Lips parted, the waitress absorbed his recital. "What's more," he emphasized, at the end, "Bigfoot swore there were never more than four in the gang, and it was just my bad luck getting tangled up with that Cottonwood heist. Claimed Dutch and the boys near busted their guts laughing when they heard I was held. Sheriff Lanker's promised he'll straighten everything out. You convinced now I'm no garroter?"

"I never did think so — really," she confessed.

"You sure acted mighty ornery," he grumbled, and unpinned his badge. "Guess I'll shuck this; I never was no great shakes as a lawman." Complacently, he added, "Guess I'll be rolling in velvet. Lanker claims I'll draw twenty percent of the value of them diamonds; then I got five thousand dollars apiece for Dutch and Bigfoot. There's plenty good graze in the hills, down below," he mused. "A feller with a little dinero could preempt a quarter-section for buildings and run all the stock he fancied." He eyed the waitress speculatively. "You fancy the idea?"

"I think it's wonderful!"

"You sticking around?"

Mildred Hogan folded her firm white arms and leaned on the counter, facing him squarely. "Guess I have to . . . you certainly need someone to keep you out of trouble."

We hope you have enjoyed this Large Print book. Other Thorndike, Wheeler, and Chivers Press Large Print books are available at your library or directly from the publishers.

For information about current and upcoming titles, please call or write, without obligation, to:

Publisher
Thorndike Press
295 Kennedy Memorial Drive
Waterville, ME 04901
Tel. (800) 223-1244

or visit our Web site at:

www.gale.com/thorndike
www.gale.com/wheeler

OR

Chivers Large Print
published by BBC Audiobooks Ltd
St James House, The Square
Lower Bristol Road
Bath BA2 3SB
England
Tel. +44(0) 800 136919
email: bbcaudiobooks@bbc.co.uk
www.bbcaudiobooks.co.uk

All our Large Print titles are designed for easy reading, and all our books are made to last.